With Friends Like These

Also by ReShonda Tate Billingsley

My Brother's Keeper
Let the Church Say Amen
Four Degrees of Heat (with Brenda L. Thomas, Crystal Lacey
Winslow, & Rochelle Alers)
I Know I've Been Changed
Have a Little Faith
Nothing But Drama
Blessings in Disguise

With Friends Like These

ReShonda Tate Billingsley

Pocket Books
New York   London   Toronto   Sydney

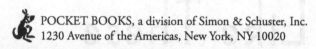 POCKET BOOKS, a division of Simon & Schuster, Inc.
1230 Avenue of the Americas, New York, NY 10020

ISBN-13: 978-1-4165-2562-2
ISBN-10:   1-4165-2562-9

This Pocket Books trade paperback edition April 2007

10 9 8 7 6 5 4 3 2 1

POCKET and colophon are registered trademarks of Simon & Schuster, Inc.

Manufactured in the United States of America

For information regarding special discounts for bulk purchases, please contact Simon & Schuster Special Sales at 1-800-456-6798 or business@simonandschuster.com

Dedicated to Mrs. Jocelyn Reed
Who dared me to dream . . .
and challenged me to follow those dreams

Acknowledgments

I can never get tired of giving thanks. That's because I have been blessed with so many wonderful people in my life, and I always want them to know how grateful I am for their continued love and support.

First and foremost, thanks to the Creator, because without God none of what I do would be possible.

To my supportive husband, Miron, thank you for everything, including the two most precious gifts I've ever received—Mya and Morgan.

To my mother, Nancy Blacknell . . . thank you for the stories. You have given me a lifetime of happiness, joy, and stories. I take back all the bad things I wished would happen to you back when I was in high school. I know now, it was all for the best.

To my little sister, Ta-Tanisha Dionne Tate . . . the wind beneath my wings. No, I'm not being corny, but you really are that breeze that keeps me going and helps me stay on the right track. Thanks for everything.

Of course, once again, I have to give much love to my agent, Sara Camilli (the absolute best in the business). And to my absolutely, positively wonderful editors, Brigitte Smith and Selena James (who helped shape this novel into what it is before she abandoned me) . . . you ladies have done wonders for my writing career and I wouldn't be where I am today if it were not for the two of you. Many, many thanks also go to Melissa Gramstad and all the other wonderful people at Simon & Schuster/Pocket Books.

To one of my closest friends, Pat Tucker Wilson, have I told you I'm proud to be your friend? Thanks for always having my back. To the talented LaWonda "LaShay" Smith, thanks for being there whenever I called. Whether it was hooking up my MySpace page, or watching the girls, I always can count on you. I must also show my appreciation to the numerous schools and churches that have had me out to share my talents and knowledge, especially Westside High School and Christa McAuliffe Middle School.

I could go on and on . . . but for the sake of creating more drama 'cuz I left someone's name out . . . let me say this: Thank you everybody and their mama! (How's that?)

Thanks to all the young people who have sent me emails, stopped me on the streets, and gone out of their way to let me know what they think about my teen books. You make all my work worthwhile. Your love and support has been so overwhelming that we're doing it again . . . keep an eye out for the next round of Good Girlz books!

Until next time, thanks for the love.

Peace.

ReShonda

(www.myspace.com/reshonda_tate_billingsley)

With Friends Like These

1

Camille

"$\mathcal{M}$y name is Tameka Adams, and I don't want to be here." Tameka made the announcement like she was at an Alcoholics Anonymous meeting. She twirled her fingers through her long ponytail as she sighed in frustration.

Personally, I wanted to tell her to beat it, then. I know one thing, if she was coming to join our group, homegirl was gon' have to lose the attitude. I mean, I know she's Rachel's niece by marriage and all. But she and her funky attitude needed to go.

Rachel is our group leader, the founder of the Good Girlz community service group. Don't let the name fool you, though. We all are far from good. Rachel started the group here in Houston as part of some youth outreach program at Zion Hill Missionary Baptist Church, where her husband was pastor. Her old snooty church members didn't want her to start the group. But even though she's First Lady, Rachel marches to a beat of her own. She told those old biddies where they could go. Now here we are, a year after we started. And even those people who didn't want us at first are now feeling us.

I ain't gon' even lie, though, I came here kickin' and screamin'. But since my choice was either the Good Girlz or jail, well, I guess you could see why I'm here. The bad part was, I got in a whole bunch of trouble over my stupid, no-good, stank, dirty dog ex-boyfriend, Keith. Long story short, the fool went to jail for a carjacking, broke out, and had me hiding him in my grandma's house. Then when the police came, he took off through a back window, and I was the one who got arrested for harboring a fugitive. Can you believe that? Me, a straight-A (well, sometimes B and C) person, got arrested. I was only fifteen, so I didn't have to go to regular jail. I spent a week in a juvenile facility while they had a manhunt for Keith. And do you know where they found that dog? At his baby mama's house. That was a bit of a problem because I didn't know he had a baby. And I dang sure didn't know he had a baby mama.

Anyway, he got sent back to jail. They eventually found out he didn't do it—it was his stepbrother—so he got out. And of course he tried to come running back to me, but I wasn't hearing it. (Okay, maybe I did take him back one time, but he messed up again, cheating on me with his crazy baby mama, so I kicked him to the curb and I hadn't talked to him since.)

"Hello. Earth to Camille."

I looked up to see Angel waving her hand in my face. I snapped back to the meeting, not even realizing my mind had wandered off.

"Glad you could rejoin us," Rachel said with a smile.

I shot her an apologetic look as she continued talking.

"Now that I've explained to our new girls all of the benefits of our wonderful group, we want everyone to introduce themselves," Rachel said. "Starting with you, Jasmine."

"Aww, Miss Rachel, it's not like Tameka doesn't know us. She's been here before," Jasmine protested. Tameka had come to our first meeting, but at the time she chose not to participate. I don't know what had brought her back this time.

"It's not like she even wants to know us," I mumbled.

Rachel must've heard me because she cut her eyes at me. "Yes, but Julia doesn't know everyone," Rachel said, referring to the brown-skinned girl sitting in the front row. "And why must you give me a hard time on everything?" Rachel asked Jasmine.

"Fine," Jasmine said. "I'm Jasmine Jones." She turned to Rachel with a huge smile. "How's that?"

Me, Alexis, and Angel cracked up laughing. Jasmine was our girl. Even though she was pretty, she used to have a complex about being so tall and athletic-looking. She'd been like Tameka when we first started, a mean tomboy who didn't want to be here. But we'd broken down her guard, and now she was totally cool. We are all tight. The only other person who'd been in our group was Alexis's friend, Trina. She joined for a little while, but got arrested for shoplifting and sent to jail. (That's another long story.) So I think none of us were too keen on anyone else joining our little circle, especially somebody with a funky attitude like Tameka.

Rachel rolled her eyes. "You all are working my nerves."

Alexis raised her hand. "I'll go, Miss Rachel. My name is Alexis Lansing," she said, standing up, tossing her long golden brown hair over her shoulder. You couldn't tell Alexis she wasn't Beyoncé's twin. Well, you could but she wouldn't believe you. "I'm a junior at St. Pius Catholic School."

"But she definitely ain't no Catholic schoolgirl," I playfully muttered, referring to her part in the little shoplifting spree she and Trina went on a few months ago. Angel high-fived me as Alexis, who was standing in front of me, shot me the finger behind her back.

"Bigmouth over here is Camille Harris," Alexis continued, pointing at me. "And that is Angel Lopez," she said, pointing at Angel. "All of them are juniors at Madison High School."

Julia gave us a smile. She was a weird-looking girl with long black hair that looked like it was in need of a good washing. She wore a long black skirt and long-sleeved black T-shirt, even though it was the middle of August.

"Now, Julia, do you want to tell us a little about yourself?" Rachel asked.

Julia shrugged. "Not much to tell. I go to Lamar High

School, and I had to come here because my friends do drugs. I don't, but my parents think I do because I hang around them. They think if I come here, it'll cure me."

We all stared at her. That girl was a druggie if I ever seen one.

"Well, even though you don't think you need to be here, maybe you'll get something out of our group," Rachel said.

Julia didn't look convinced. But Rachel didn't seem to notice as she began talking about all the community service projects we would be working on, including the one we had scheduled for Saturday.

By the time we wrapped up, I think all of us were worn out. Alexis, Angel, and Jasmine immediately gravitated toward one another, so I decided to personally welcome Julia and Tameka, who were sitting off by themselves.

"Hey, are you guys going to be at the community service project Saturday?" I asked.

Tameka folded her arms and stuck out her bottom lip. "I guess, since it seems like we don't really have a choice."

Julia rolled her eyes. "Not if I can help it."

The three of us stood there, looking around awkwardly. I noticed Angel, Alexis, and Jasmine cracking up about something. Finally, when I saw neither Julia or Tameka were in a talkative mood, I shrugged. "Oh, well. See you guys later." I went back to my friends, telling myself I'd tried. I'd just stick to the original Good Girlz, the ones I knew were my true friends. I guess we just had no room for outsiders.

2

Alexis

I can't believe I ate so much. My stomach feels like if I hiccupped, it would explode." Jasmine rubbed her stomach as she leaned back in the seat.

I shook my head at her. It just didn't make sense to eat like a pig. I tried to tell her that, but of course, she wasn't listening to me.

We were leaving Jasmine's favorite restaurant, the Golden Corral. As far as she was concerned, no restaurant in town could compare to the all-you-can eat buffet.

I was dropping Jasmine off in front of her apartment complex. Tameka had gone home with Rachel and Julia was a no-show at this morning's community service project. We'd gone to the Julia C. Hester House, a senior citizens' center, and played bingo with the residents. It wasn't the way I'd prefer to spend my Saturday morning, but it hadn't been as bad as I thought it would be.

Angel and Camille were in the back seat, stuffed as well.

I was the only one who didn't look like I was about to pass out. Probably because I had only eaten a salad. Jasmine had said that made no sense to her.

"Why go to an all-you-can eat buffet if all you're gonna eat is lettuce?" she'd asked.

They just didn't understand. I may have been slim and trim now, but I was a straight butterball just two years ago. People don't even believe it, but I weighed two hundred pounds by the eighth grade. It was horrible, and my mother tripped all the time, which only depressed me and made me eat even more.

But luckily, I took up running and started loving it. I ran every chance I got, and the weight just started dropping off.

"Hey, what's going on over there?" Camille said as she leaned up and pointed at the basketball court in front of Jasmine's apartment complex.

"Oh, that's all the guys around here and their Saturday-afternoon basketball game," Jasmine replied nonchalantly.

"Oooooh, looks like a lot of cute guys over there," Camille said, swooning.

"Yeah, right." Jasmine turned up her nose. "You don't want any of these bustas from my neighborhood."

"Can I just look, dang?" Camille smiled. Jasmine shook her head at Camille's boy-crazy behind.

"I'm with Camille," Angel said, leaning up as well. "Let's go look."

"Bet," I said as I pulled into a parking spot in front of Jasmine's apartment. I shut off the car and grabbed some lip gloss. I dabbed it on my lips before passing it on to Camille and Angel, who did the same.

Jasmine groaned as we started climbing out of the car. "Y'all act like you ain't never seen no boys before," she mumbled.

"Look, just because you got your nose wide open behind Donovan, don't hate on us," Camille joked.

"Whatever." Jasmine waved Camille off, but I couldn't help but notice the smile that crept up on her face. I knew she was thinking about her boyfriend, Donovan. He graduated this past May and was now away at college. Personally, I didn't know how they handled a long-distance relationship, but Jasmine seemed cool with it.

Camille was about to say something, but her eyes lit up at the sight of all the shirtless boys running up and down the basketball court, so whatever she was about to say must have no longer been important.

"Girl, look at that dark-skinned one right there," Camille said as she walked over and grabbed my arm. "He is so fine."

"Ewwww," Jasmine said as she walked up behind us. "That's Ricky. He calls himself Pretty Ricky. That alone should tell you something."

"Shoot, I see why he calls himself that," Camille said, eyeing him up and down.

Angel nodded. "You got that right. But I'm checking out the one over there in the white Nike tank."

We all turned toward a short curly-haired boy who was taking a swig from his Gatorade bottle.

"You would choose the shortest one on the court," Camille laughed.

"Whatever," Angel responded, running her fingers through her long, wavy black hair. "Short or not, he is too cute."

"That's Jose. And he has a baby," Jasmine responded.

"Ummm, so do I," Angel said. "So we could have a ready-made family." She grinned.

"Don't make me throw up," Jasmine said. "You think Marcus is a deadbeat dad," she said, referring to Angel's baby's father, who didn't want to have anything to do with her or their child. "Jose's son is nine, and Jose still won't claim him."

Angel turned up her nose, like she'd suddenly lost interest in him. "Unh-unh. I definitely don't want a deadbeat dad."

"Jasmine, I don't believe you've been holding out on us like this. This is where we should've been hanging out," Camille said as she continued to look around the basketball court.

"I know," I added. "All this fineness up in one area. Like, oh my God." I stopped talking and put my hand to my chest. "I think I'm in love," I said as I stared at the court. "That is the finest boy on the face of the planet, and he needs to be my next boyfriend."

Jasmine closed her eyes and shook her head. "Girl, please. You don't know any of these boys. Ain't none of them boyfriend material. I don't even know who you are talking about. But I know the boys in my neighborhood, and none of them are people I'd fix my friends up with."

"Who are you talking about?" Camille asked.

I grabbed Angel's arm. "Oh, my God. He's walking over here."

We all looked at a group of boys who were walking toward us. They were high-fiving each other, I guess because they had won their game.

"The one with the basketball," I said.

Jasmine looked toward the boys and her mouth dropped open. "Double, triple, quadruple ewwww."

"Girl, please. You can not tell me he ain't fine," I whispered, lowering my voice.

"Yes, I really can," Jasmine said as the group walked right up to us.

"What's up, Jasmine?" Ricky said. "Who are your friends?"

"You don't know them," she said with an attitude.

"That's the problem," Ricky said, looking at Camille like she was T-bone steak and he was a starving dog.

"Boy, beat it," Jasmine said, flicking him off.

Ricky laughed and turned toward the boy with the basketball. "Jaquan, why yo sister so mean?"

"Mean queen, that's Jasmine," Jaquan replied.

"You not gon' introduce us to your friends?" another one of the boys said.

"No, Kelvin, I'm not," Jasmine replied. She looked over at me. I know I was still standing there with my mouth hanging open.

"Don't be like that," Ricky said.

"Hey, fools, we need to do the best outta three! Where y'all goin'?" Some boy yelled from the basketball court.

All of the guys turned toward the yelling.

"We gotta have a tie-breaker game," the boy shouted as he threw his arms up in the air.

"So these bustas ain't had enough, huh?" Ricky said, laughing and shaking his head. "Let's go again."

"A'wight, man," Jaquan shouted to the boy. "Here we come." He turned back toward his friends. "Come on, y'all."

Ricky smiled at Camille one more time. "Bye, baby. Hope I see you around," he said, licking his lips.

"I hope you do, too," Camille sweetly said as he took off toward the court.

"Y'all are goin' to make me throw up, for real," Jasmine said, turning and heading off the court.

I jumped in front of Jasmine. "Oh, no, you don't. Why did you not tell me that fine thing was your brother?"

"I'm sorry, I would have no earthly idea what fine thing you're talking about," Jasmine coolly replied. "Because you couldn't possibly be talking about Jaquan. Besides, you saw him at the banquet last year."

I leaned back and looked at Jaquan again. He did look familiar, but I would've definitely remembered somebody that cute.

Jasmine shook her head. "He was a lot shorter and a lot nerdier looking. He just sprouted up over the summer. Now he thinks he all fine and stuff."

"He is." I glanced toward the court again. "Hook a sista up."

"First of all, the slang. Not you," Jasmine said, wagging her finger side to side in my face. "Second of all, I really do like you. And since I wouldn't fix my brother up with my worst enemy, that's not an option. Got it?"

"Nope," I replied with a smile. "He's the one."

"You don't even know him. He's a jerk."

"You're just saying that because you don't want me to talk to him," I responded.

Jasmine sighed. She should've known I wasn't trying to hear anything she had to say.

"So, will you stop being my friend if I talk to your brother?" I asked as I cocked my head at her.

"Huh? Of course not. But I'm just trying to tell you—"

I cut her off. "Then the only thing I ask is that you tell your brother to call me."

Jasmine looked at me like I was on drugs. "I can't stop you from talking to Jaquan, but I dang sure ain't gon' help you. And if you know like I know, you'd stay as far away from my got-a-different-girlfriend-every-week brother."

I ignored Jasmine as I took another look at Jaquan's cute self. Yep, I was determined to get to know her brother a little bit better—with or without her help.

3

Camille

Rachel was bouncing off the walls. She was so excited, she could barely contain herself.

"Miss Rachel, are you going to tell us what's going on or what?" I said. Her excitement had me curious. We were at our weekly Tuesday meeting, but instead of talking about community service or Bible lessons, Rachel had said she had a major announcement.

She smiled as she looked out the door. "I told you all it was a surprise. One I'm sure you'll love."

I took my seat up front, bracing myself for Rachel's surprise.

"Okay, quiet, quiet," she said as she stood at the front of the room. By the time Tameka, Jasmine, Julia, Angel, and Alexis had all shuffled to their seats, I was about to lose my mind with anticipation.

"One of Zion Hill's faithful members, Shereen Young, has an incredible opportunity for you girls. Shereen works at Channel 2, and today she's joining us to make a very special announcement. I'd like you all to give her your undivided attention, and please save your questions until she's finished." Rachel looked around the room. "Okay, it looks like everyone is ready. Let me go and bring her in."

The minute Rachel left her post at the front of the room, the whispering started. Everyone was more than just a little curious about this "surprise."

Rachel stepped back in the room, accompanied by a beautiful, heavyset woman who was wearing a long flowing skirt and ruffled sleeveless blouse. Her sandy brown hair was in a curly Afro.

"Hello, everyone," Shereen said. "As I'm sure Rachel has told you, my name is Shereen. I have been a fan of the Good Girlz program since its inception."

We all looked on, still trying to figure out what was going on.

"I'm glad to be here with you today," she continued, looking at Rachel. "Thanks for giving me this time to speak with your girls." She turned her attention back to us. "I'm here on behalf of my station, KPCR, Channel 2. We are doing a new show called *Teen Talks*, and I'm heading up the new program designed to target issues facing teens today. We had a host scheduled to start in two weeks, and because of circumstances beyond our control, she simply will not be able to do it. That puts us in a bad situation, as we're scheduled to start taping in a couple of weeks. So I've been charged with finding a new host for the show, quickly. We're looking for just the right person to bring excitement, talent, and personality to the program."

A huge grin crossed my face. I looked around the room. Everyone, including Tameka, looked as excited as I was. Well, except for Julia. She kept her same weird look. We all started talking and asking a bunch of questions.

"Settle down. I'll answer all of your questions in a minute," Shereen said. "But I need to add that not only would you host the show, which will tape once a week in the evenings, but the job also pays five hundred dollars a week."

That made all of our eyes get even bigger.

"I've been trying to find the best way to go about finding the perfect host," Shereen said. "And since I'm a faithful member of Zion Hill, I decided to start here. You ladies have the first shot."

"Wow!" I said. "That is so cool."

Shereen smiled as she folded her arms and nodded. "We think so."

All I could think was that she was speaking directly to me. I could see myself now in that position as the host of this new teen show. I immediately started thinking about all the great ideas I'd come up with.

"So, are there any questions?" she asked.

Every hand in the room flew into the air. I was honestly

too mesmerized by the idea of being able to host my own show on TV. I had questions, but my real question was how I could get the job. That's all I was really concerned with. Besides, I had a feeling Angel and Alexis or even Jasmine would ask enough questions.

"So, what do we have to do?" Alexis asked.

"Well, there is an audition process," Shereen continued. "And because you'll be a role model of sorts in this position, we do ask that you be passing all of your classes."

"That's no problem for my girls," Rachel stepped in and said. "Everyone is passing, right?"

We all nodded.

"So, what will you be looking for?" Tameka asked, finally seeming to lose the attitude she'd had since day one.

"We're looking for a host with personality. One who can draw the viewers in and keep the show moving along," Shereen said.

"When do we get to audition?" I was so excited. I already wanted to be a television news reporter when I grew up, so this was right up my alley.

"Well, there are three rounds of auditions you'll have to go through. The first will be a basic on-air test to make sure you even have what it takes to host a show. Some people freeze up on camera, or know this is something they could never do. We don't want to waste their time or ours. So I guess that would be my first question. Anyone in here not interested in hosting the show?"

We all looked around the room. Julia, who was sitting in the back of the room, slowly raised her hand. "Actually, I won't be able to do it. This is my last meeting. My parents are moving to Ohio."

"Oh, I'm sorry to hear that," Rachel said.

We all looked like we could care less—probably because no one really knew her, and she definitely hadn't made an effort to get to know us.

Julia shrugged like it was no big deal.

I didn't mean to sound cold, but I had too many questions to be worrying about Julia. "I think we all are excited about the opportunity," I said.

"Actually," Angel interrupted me, "as much as I would love to take part, and I dang sure could use the money, my mom works in the evening. And I know with the baby, I just can't do it. But I'm definitely here to help my girls out." She playfully pushed my shoulder.

"Well, that settles it, then," Shereen said. "We have four candidates for the job. Now, I have to tell you, if myself and the other producers don't think any of you is the person we're looking for, we will open the search up to other Houston-area teens."

"You won't have to look anywhere else," I bragged.

"That's right, because you've found your new host right here," Tameka said, pointing to her chest. "Television is in my blood. My cousin is a reporter for CNN."

I cut a sideways glance at her. She sure was arrogant all of a sudden. She'd barely said two words since we first met, and now she was all cocky.

"Not," Alexis joked. "I would say the Teen Talks host is right here." She stood up and took a bow.

Jasmine stood up next to Alexis and bumped her with her hips. "You mean right here." She patted her chest.

We all laughed, except for Tameka. She looked like she might be taking this a little too seriously.

"All right. Settle down, girls. Let Shereen finish telling you how the audition will work," Rachel said.

Everybody took their seats.

"I'm glad to see such enthusiasm," Shereen said. "We'll do the on-air test next week. That will be followed by a round of interviews with the producers, and then you'll actually tape a show." She started passing out some papers. "If you all would, please, fill out this application and bring it with you to the on-air test, which will be held at the Channel 2 studios on next Friday."

Shereen answered a few more questions before heading out.

"I trust that you all will represent me well," Rachel said after she was gone.

"And you know this," I playfully said.

"And I'm not going to support this unless we all agree this will be a friendly competition," Rachel added.

"Of course," I said. Everyone else nodded as well.

After we wrapped up that conversation, Alexis stood up, looking at her watch. "We'll be all set, Miss Rachel, but for now we have to go. We're all working a catering event for my dad."

"Not all of us," Tameka said.

I raised my eyebrows. Alexis's father had asked us to help out as waitresses at some business event tonight when his caterers found themselves short-staffed. Alexis had immediately called me, Angel, and Jasmine. I bet she forgot to call Tameka and Julia.

"I'm so sorry," Alexis said. "I wasn't even thinking, Tameka. I'm sure it won't be a problem for you to help, too."

Tameka stood and grabbed her purse. "No, thanks. Since I'm just an afterthought and all, I'll just go on home and start practicing for my audition."

She turned up her nose as she walked out of the room. While I desperately wanted the *Teen Talks* job, if it didn't go to me, I'd rather it went to anybody but Tameka.

4

Camille

This money was burning a hole in my pocket. Alexis's dad had given us all two hundred dollars for working his business event. My mom had made me save a hundred dollars—talking about a rainy day. Shoot, the way the rain was pouring down around us right about now, I'd tried to convince her it was a rainy day. Of course, she wasn't hearing it and told me I'd better get out of her face before she took the other hundred.

I rounded up my girls, and they were just as geeked as I was to get to the mall. Jasmine was the only one who wasn't anxious to spend her money. She was talking about how she wanted to put her money up. I guess that's because she probably hadn't seen two hundred dollars in her life. Her family was dirt-poor. We'd convinced her to do like me and put one hundred up and come with us to the mall. She'd done so reluctantly, but now that she was here, she was like a kid in the candy store. Alexis, on the other hand, had looked at the money like it was no big deal.

"You can't buy nothing with two hundred dollars," she'd griped.

"You might not be able to, but I dang sure can," Jasmine had replied. "And if it's no big deal to you, gimme your part." Jasmine held her hand out. Alexis laughed and shook her head.

We were now making our way through First Colony Mall. I had to pull Jasmine away from Foot Locker because when we'd met her, she dressed like a boy, in warm-ups and tennis shoes. Now that we'd gotten her to dress somewhat like a young lady, we wanted to keep her that way.

"Oh, Donovan would love you in that," I said to Jasmine as we stopped and looked in the window of Forever 21. She looked at the aqua dress I was pointing at.

"Dang, that's tight," Jasmine replied.

"As microbraids," Alexis said.

We all looked at her.

"You are so corny." Jasmine laughed.

Alexis gave her the hand. "Don't hate, appreciate."

"We told you about those busta sayings," I replied.

We looked around, noticing Angel wasn't around. "Hey, where did Angel go?"

"Where else?" Jasmine said, pointing to Children's Place across the mall.

I felt kinda sad for a minute. Angel's daughter Angelica

was almost a year old now. She'd made it clear that when she got her money, she couldn't spend it on herself. She had to buy her daughter some clothes because she was always growing. That was jacked up, but I guess that was what motherhood was all about. I didn't even want to know about that until I was like thirty-something.

"I hate that Angel can't at least buy herself something," I said as I watched Angel sift through the clearance rack in the children's store. "She really—" I stopped talking as I turned to Alexis and Jasmine. They had turned around and were staring at one of the most gorgeous guys I'd ever laid eyes on. He was tall, sandpaper brown, had a tight fade, and his Sean Johns hung just enough to be sexy but not enough to be a turnoff. He was in the music store with some headphones on, bobbing his head to whatever it was he was listening to.

"Oh. My. God," I said.

"You can say that again," Alexis said.

"Oh. My. God," I repeated.

"Okay, he's almost as fine as Donovan," Jasmine said.

I stared at the boy. "Naw, boo. I know Donovan is fine as all get-out, but that is fine, with a capital F."

The boy turned and looked out the window, catching us staring at him. We giggled and quickly looked away. I bet we looked so stupid standing out in the middle of the mall giggling like we were in junior high or something. He held up his hand, I guess asking us to wait. He motioned to someone else in the store and headed toward the door.

"Jasmine, you have a man," I whispered. "So move. This one is between me and Alexis."

Jasmine shook her head. "Y'all need some medication to cure that boy craziness."

The boy came walking toward us, followed by another guy who must've been his friend. His friend could've stayed in the store. He had to be a good four hundred pounds. Then the gold around his neck had to add another fifty pounds.

Me and Alexis smiled as the guys approached us. We grinned and put on our sophisticated-girl looks.

"Can we come hang out with y'all? 'Cause shisters be looking finnnnnneeee," the cute one said.

I don't know whose smile faded first, mine or Alexis's.

"Shisters?" I said.

The big boy laughed. "He's trying to say sisters. My boy got a small speech impediment."

"Shisters. That's what I said," he repeated.

I looked at him crazy. "It's sisters. No *h*."

"And that's not the only thing he's got," Alexis said as she took a step back and fanned her hand in front of her face. "Good grief. Have you been eating garlic or something?"

It was his turn to look crazy. "Huh? My breath stank?"

"So much that it should be a crime," I said, taking a step back myself.

His boys started laughing as he covered his mouth and nose and blew into his hand.

"Whatever," he said, after smelling his hand. "You trying to be funny."

I wanted to tell him, really I'm not, but I didn't want to be any more rude than we'd already been.

"Yo, I'm Big T," the big guy said as he took a step forward. "This is Luscious D."

"Are y'all rappers or something?" Jasmine asked, finally stepping into the conversation.

"Naw, that's just our names," Big T replied. "'Cause I'm big, and my boy is luscious."

Jasmine stared at him for a minute. "Don't ever, ever, ever tell anybody that again." She turned and walked away, shaking her head.

"Sho, what's the deal," Luscious said, stepping toward me again. "Y'all gon' let us hang out with y'all or what? I got a pocketful of money, and I figured we could shwing by Applebee's or shomething."

I stepped back again. It didn't make any sense that such good looks were wasted on somebody like him.

"You need to *shwing* by a speech therapist," Jasmine said, rolling her eyes. I hit her with my elbow, and she shook her head again as she went and sat down.

"Well, look here," I said, as I stepped out of the way to let some people pass. "We'd love to hang out with you guys, but, ummm"—I looked around, trying to figure out how we could get these guys away from us. "Our boyfriends wouldn't like that."

Alexis looked at me funny.

"Boyfriends? They don't have to know," Luscious said.

"Well, ummm, they're here at the mall with us," I said as I looked around nervously. I know Jasmine was wondering why I didn't just tell them we weren't interested and move on. But while she was the mean one, I did try not to hurt people's feelings too bad.

I guess Alexis finally caught on. "Yeah, so we'd better get going. See ya, 'bye." She grabbed my arm and pulled me away.

We walked a couple of steps and looked up to see Luscious D and Big T following us.

"I don't shee no boyfriends," Luscious said, looking around.

Jasmine rolled her eyes, and me and Alexis tried to keep from busting out laughing. We looked up at three guys walking out of the Eddie Bauer store. I made eye contact with one of the guys. He smiled, and I took that as my opportunity. "Hey, baby," I said as I walked quickly over to the tallest of the three. I wrapped my arm through his. "We've been looking all over for you guys."

Everyone, the guy included, looked at me like I had lost my mind.

"Sorry, guys," I told Luscious and Big T. "But as I was saying, our boyfriends are waiting on us."

Alexis smiled, I guess finally catching on. That girl could be so slow sometimes. She walked over and took one of the other boy's hands. That one, who looked like he couldn't be any more than five feet tall, broke out in a huge smile as he leaned back and looked at Alexis's butt. The third boy looked at Jasmine and grinned. Jasmine folded her arms. "My boyfriend is at home," she said.

I tried to ignore Jasmine and scooted in closer to my boyfriend-for-the-moment.

"Y'all with these fools?" Luscious said.

While our three new friends didn't seem like the rough type, they didn't seem like punks either. Especially the one I was with.

"Excuse me," the boy I was with said as he stepped toward them. "I think the young ladies told you all they were with us, so we'd appreciate it if you kept moving."

Luscious looked at Big T. "You hear that, T? They'd appreciate it if we kept moving." Luscious was about to say something else as a snarl crossed his face. Luckily, Big T must've noticed the security guards walking toward us, because he grabbed Luscious's arm. "Yo, man. Let's roll. They ain't even worth it." He motioned toward the guard, and that quickly got Luscious's attention because, without saying another word, he spun around and walked off.

I smiled at my boyfriend-for-the-moment. "Hey, thanks a bunch for helping us out. Sorry to throw you out there like that, but we were desperate to get rid of those bustas."

"No problem," he said as he stuck out his hand. "I'm Walter Lewis."

I shook it. "I'm Camille Harris. This is Alexis and Jasmine," I said, pointing to my girls.

"Well, my vertically challenged friend here is Sam, and that's Elbert," Walter said, motioning toward his other friend.

"El," Elbert said, cutting his eyes at Walter. "My friends call me El."

Sam looked at Alexis with that big goofy grin still across his face. "I'll be your boyfriend for real."

Alexis turned up her nose. "Thanks, but I have a boyfriend already," she lied.

"Bet he isn't as fine as me," Sam said, sticking out his puny chest. Alexis looked like she was trying not to throw up.

Me and Walter laughed. Jasmine rolled her eyes like she was ready to go.

"So, if both your girls have a boyfriend, I'm sure you do, too," Walter said as he stared into my eyes.

I felt my stomach flutter. "Actually, I'm very much single." I hadn't really had a boyfriend since Keith, the guy I'd gotten into all that trouble behind.

"Well, Camille, I would really like to take you out sometimes. Maybe to a movie or something." Walter smiled, his dimples melting my heart.

I smiled back, surprised that I was even considering going out with him. "Sure," I finally said.

He pulled out his cell phone and programmed my number in. "I will definitely give you a call."

"Do that," I said, trying to sound cute.

I waved as he walked off. I turned to see both Alexis and Jasmine standing there with their arms crossed. "Could you be any more desperate?" Jasmine said.

"Desperate? How you figure that?"

"You know you don't want that boy," Jasmine snapped.

"And why wouldn't I? Because he's white?" I responded.

"Ummm, yeah," Jasmine said.

"And? Alexis is half white," I said defensively.

"I'm not half of anything. I'm multiracial. My mother is white and black and my father is from the Dominican Republic," she proudly proclaimed.

"Okay, Tiger Woods." I laughed.

"If you look black, you are black," Jasmine said. "And you ain't gon' have nothing but problems trying to date a white boy."

"That's one of the dumbest things I've ever heard you say," I responded. "Besides, what difference does it make? He's cute. That's all that matters."

Jasmine threw her hands up as she walked off. "Whatever. If you like it, I love it."

I watched as Walter made his way down the mall. I smiled. I definitely liked it, and couldn't wait to get to know Walter Lewis a little bit better.

5

Alexis

𝒥asmine looked at me like she was trying to figure out why I was standing at her door.

"What? You weren't expecting me?" I flashed a big, cheesy grin.

"No, I thought you were those pesky kids from down the hall. They're always trying to sell something—magazines, chocolate bars, cookies, anything to make a dime," she said.

"Nope, not selling anything." I shifted my weight, anxious to get inside. "Are you gon' let me in or what?"

Jasmine stepped aside and let me walk in. "I didn't know you were coming over. I thought you said you had to study for that calculus test. What's up?" she said.

My gaze danced around the room. "I didn't feel like studying." I didn't want to come right out and tell her the real reason I was there because I really didn't know if she was going to trip. But when Jaquan walked into the living room, slowly sipping on a glass of Sunny Delight, I think it became obvious why I was there, especially from the way both of our eyes lit up.

"Hey, Alexis. What's up?" He flashed a lopsided smile. I hadn't told anyone, but I called Jaquan earlier this week when I knew Jasmine wasn't home. I'd acted like I was calling for her, and I was so grateful that he answered. Instead of hanging up after he told me Jasmine wasn't in, he talked to me for almost an hour. I was excited that he even remembered me from the basketball court. But he'd said, "As pretty as you are, who wouldn't remember you?"

I was hooked from that moment. We had talked every day since then, and he'd invited me over today just to hang out.

Jasmine turned toward her brother and frowned. "What do you want?" She turned up her nose and sniffed. "And did you have to take a bath in that cologne? Sheesh," she grumbled.

Jaquan ignored her and walked toward me. "I'm glad you could make it."

Jasmine's eyes got big. She looked at me. "What is he talking about?"

"Me and Alexis 'bout to roll out." He took my hand. I tried not to blush.

"Roll out?" Jasmine said. "You're here for him?" She looked at Jaquan like she thought somebody was playing a joke on her. "Y'all serious? So what, y'all talking now?"

"And so what if we are?" Jaquan said. "Come on, let's go," he told me. "We're taking your car, right?" I nodded and handed him my keys. My dad would have a heart attack, but I didn't care.

Jasmine's draw dropped open. "You letting him drive your BMW?"

Now she was starting to sound like my mom.

"Jasmine, why don't you stay outta my business," Jaquan said.

"Alexis is my friend. So this is my business," she shot back.

I definitely didn't want to see them fighting over me. "Hey, Jaquan, let me talk to Jasmine just for a minute," I said.

He let out a frustrated sigh. "Fine. Meet me on the basketball court. I'ma go holla at one of my boys. Don't be long." Jaquan then leaned over and gently kissed me on the lips. It caught me off guard. But when he looked at Jasmine and laughed, I knew he was just trying to get under her skin. Even still, the kiss sent goose bumps up my arm.

As soon as Jaquan left, Jasmine spun on me. "What in the world is wrong with you? Why are you messing with my brother?"

"I told you, Jasmine. I like him. He likes me. What's the big deal?"

"So, what's gon' happen when y'all break up? What's gon' happen if he cheats on you? Or you cheat on him? I don't wanna be caught up in the middle of no mess."

"Nobody is cheating on nobody, okay. We just kickin' it," I tried to reason.

"No, it's not okay," she said as she folded her arms across her chest.

I took a deep breath. "Well, it's gon' have to be okay. Because me and Jaquan are together."

"Oh, y'all together now?" Jasmine cocked her head. "'Cuz, I don't think he kn—" Jasmine threw her hands up. "You know what? Forget it. You do what you wanna do."

We stared each other down for a minute. I didn't want to go there with Jasmine, but she couldn't dictate who I could and couldn't see. "I will go there, Jasmine," I finally said. "And what I wanna do is be with Jaquan. So I'm gonna be with Jaquan." I turned and headed toward the door.

"Just leave me out of it," she called out as I headed out the door. "No matter what happens, leave me out of it!"

I let the front door slam on the sound of her voice.

6

Camille

I twirled the phone cord around my finger. Today was a good day. We had the day off from school and I was stretched out across my bed, going into my third hour of talking to Walter. I probably should have been studying for my history test on Monday, but my conversations with Walter were so much more fun.

"So, did you see Taylor from *American Idol* last night on Jay Leno?" he asked.

"Nah, I don't watch Jay Leno. My mom says ever since Arsenio Hall went off, she stopped watching late-night TV, so we never really watch it."

"Who is Arsenio Hall?"

"I don't know. Somebody who used to have a popular talk show, I guess. My mom is always raving about how funny he was," I replied. "But I like Taylor, even though I'm still surprised he won. Personally, I was rooting for

Paris. I'm surprised you even know who Taylor is, though. You don't seem like the *American Idol* type." Walter was one of the smartest guys I'd ever met. Since I met him in the mall last week, we'd talked almost daily. He had me laughing all the time. I was especially impressed with the fact that he got straight A's and had already been accepted to Princeton. But I guess that shouldn't really surprise me, since his father was a state senator and his mother was a former Miss Texas.

"I only watch the show because my sister is a die-hard fan," he said, snapping me back to our conversation.

"So is my friend Alexis." I laughed.

"Was she the one at the mall with you?" he asked.

"Yeah, the one Sam was trying to talk to."

Walter laughed, and we started talking about something else. After a few minutes he asked me to hold on a minute. When he returned to the phone, he said, "So you ever been to a drive-in movie?"

"Nope, never have. I mean, I've seen some in movies, and I even saw on the news last week about this new one that opened up between here and San Antonio, but I've never been to one before," I said.

"Hmm, well, looks like I may have to take you, then. We could go with a few of our friends and make a road trip out of it. I think you'll like it."

"Really?" I asked. I thought there was no way my mom

was letting me go on a road trip with a boy, even if it was
with a group of people.

"Man, it is so much fun. We used to go to the one near
Gatesville when I lived in Killeen. My dad was stationed
there for close to fifteen years. It was off the chart," he said
excitedly.

I just loved how his slang seemed so natural, not like a
white boy trying to be black, like this guy named Mark at
my school.

"Sounds like fun," I said. "So y'all would just pile up
into a car and go to the drive-in, huh? But what about
privacy?" I asked.

"You don't think about that when you're at the drive-
in. I mean, either you're in a minivan, which is way cool,
or—"

"A minivan?" I balked.

"Well, I'm just telling you what some people used to
do. Me, well, I'd hop into my dad's Chevy Impala and
bring along a couple of big thick blankets. Talk about a
proper drive-in date experience. Now that's what I'm talking 'bout." He chuckled.

I was thinking about the picture he was painting for me.
I started getting all excited thinking about me, Angel, and
Jasmine, with our dates, of course. Yeah, that would be tight.

"You sold me. So whassup? When can we go?" At this
point, I'd go to the moon with Walter. Even if it meant
having to lie to my mom.

"You serious?" he asked, sounding all surprised.

"Yeah, let me talk to my girls and we can plan a group trip."

"Okay, cool, that sounds good."

Suddenly a voice rang through, interrupting our conversation.

"Walter, are you still on the phone?"

"Um, yes, ma'am," he said.

"I need to use it, sweetheart," she said.

"Okay, Ma. Let me just say 'bye to my girl. I'll call you when we're off," he answered.

I started feeling all warm and tingly inside. He had just referred to me as "his girl" to his mother. Yeah, things were really starting to take off between us.

I was glad he couldn't see me blushing. I don't know why he had my stomach fluttering and stuff. I had never been remotely attracted to a guy of another race, but the funny thing was I didn't see any color when it came to Walter. I just saw a really cute guy who I enjoyed talking to.

"Look, Camille, my mom needs the phone, but I really want to take you out. I mean, I know we're gonna do the drive-in thing, but I mean before then. We could like go to TGI Friday's or something. How does that sound?"

"Sounds like a plan," I replied.

"You wanna go tomorrow?" he asked.

I bit my lip. "Dang, I can't. We're having a sleepover at Alexis's."

"So, we'll go tonight. I'll pick you up around six. Where do you live?"

I sat up in the bed. "Today?"

He laughed. "What better time than the present? Is that cool with you?"

I glanced over at the digital clock on my nightstand. It was already three o'clock. Then there was my mother to deal with. She wasn't going to be happy about me going out with someone she didn't know. But shoot, if I didn't go tonight, I'd have to wait till next week. "Why don't I just meet you at six at the restaurant?"

"What, you're ashamed of me?" he joked.

"Boy, please," I laughed. "It's just my mom isn't even going to be feeling me going out with a stranger."

"I'm not a stranger."

"You know what I mean."

He laughed. "I know. That's cool. I'll meet you at six at the Friday's by First Colony Mall."

We said our good-byes, and I sat in bed wondering what I would say to my mother. I had really tried to get away from lying to her, but I didn't see any other way out of it.

I jumped up from my bed and made my way down the hall to my mother's bedroom. I softly knocked on her door.

"Hey, Ma," I said as I eased into the room. She was sitting in her chaise lounge with her reading glasses on, her head buried deep in her Bible.

"Hello, sweetheart," she said, looking up at me. "I thought you were taking a nap."

I walked over to her bed. "Nah, just in my room hanging out."

She smiled at me, and I felt a twinge of guilt about the lie that was about to come out of my mouth. Me and my mom had been through some serious drama over the past year, and we were finally getting back on track. I hated to mess all that up by lying to her, but I knew my mother. No way would she let me go out with a boy she'd never even heard me talk about.

I took a deep breath. "Hey, we're going to have a sleepover at Alexis's tonight."

"I thought the sleepover was tomorrow night," my mother said as she removed her glasses.

"Yeah, but we have another community service project we need to work out all the details for, and tomorrow is all for the kids we're mentoring," I lied. I had already figured it out. I would hang out with Walter until he had to go, then I'd come home and tell my mother that I wasn't feeling good and had to come home.

"Oh, well, then you have fun," she said.

I flashed a smile and headed toward the door. I stopped just before I left and turned to my mother. "I'm going to leave around five-thirty, if that's okay."

My mother nodded. "Yes, sweetheart. You have fun and remember, I love you."

I swear, my mother gave me this sweet look that made me want to go running back into her room, begging her to forgive me for lying. But images of Walter kept me from coming clean.

I swallowed, waved to my mom and said, "I love you, too. I'll be careful." Then I headed to my room to start getting ready for my date.

7

Camille

$\mathcal{I}$ was trying my best not to get impatient while Walter stood yapping on his cell phone.

"Hey, man, if my mom or dad calls, just tell them I'm in the bathroom or something. Yeah, man, that's all I need you to do. I'll be there," he said.

We had met in the parking lot of TGI Friday's. I wasn't gon' interrupt, but I could tell that just like me, he had to lie to his folks to see me. I wish parents understood that telling us no only makes us want to see each other even more.

"Nah, I don't think they're gonna call, I'm just saying if they do, that's all." Walter shook his head as if his friend could see him. "Yeah, cool, I'll meet you at your house, but I'll call you when I'm ready, okay?"

The minute he got off the phone, I said, "So, what was that all about?"

He shrugged off my question at first. But I guess the look on my face told him he couldn't just blow me off.

"Oh, that's nothing," he finally said. "My mother trips sometimes. After I told her you were my girl, she started talking 'bout I'm too young to be serious with anyone. She claims we have a plan—college, grad school, then a serious girlfriend. So rather than deal with her, I just let her think I'm with her plan."

I didn't say anything as I followed him inside the restaurant. We put our name on the waiting list and were standing off to the side when Walter's cell phone rang again. I bit my lips, but didn't say anything. I hoped his phone wouldn't ring all evening.

"You coming over here?" I heard him ask. He paused. "Yeah, we're 'bout to be seated, then we were talking about catching a nine o'clock movie. We can meet you there. Cool."

He snapped his phone shut, then turned to me. "I hope you don't mind, but I told Sam him and his girl could meet us at the movies."

I faked like I was pouting. Although I was just playing, I really did want our first date to just be us.

"Aww, c'mon, there's nothing wrong with having a little company tag along with us." He playfully pinched my chin. "Besides, we'll talk about all the private stuff over dinner, long before the movie starts, anyway."

I smiled. "I was just kidding, I don't mind. But you still

didn't tell me what's up with your folks. I mean, what do they have against me?"

"It's nothing like that at all. I mean, they don't know you. I'm telling you, my mother is just afraid I'll get all wrapped up in some girl and my grades will fall, and all that stupid stuff. Nothing for you to worry about, though. I got them under control." Walter took his arm and threw it over my shoulder, pulling me closer.

By the time they called us to our table, I was afraid Walter could hear my stomach growling. That's just how hungry I was.

At the table, we ordered, laughed, and talked until our food arrived. I loved the way things with us just seemed so natural. We were just finishing up dinner when we heard a voice say, "So, now you're in the business of lying to your mother."

Walter's eyes got huge as he jumped up. "Mom!"

"Don't mom me." His mother folded her arms. She was a very elegant-looking woman, with beautiful blond hair that hung loosely around her face. She looked like she couldn't have been a day over thirty and was dressed like she was someone important in some navy linen capris and a cream tank. "I was leaving Pier One, and I thought that was your car over here," she said. "Since you were supposed to be at Sam's studying, I came in here to see for myself if my son had turned into a liar."

"Mom, are you following me?" Walter asked.

"Follow you? Son, I don't have to follow you. Or at least, I didn't think I needed to follow you." She must've finally decided to acknowledge me, because she turned to me, her nose in the air. "So, are you the reason my son has taken to lying?"

I stood up myself, not wanting her first impression of me to be a negative one. "I'm Camille." I stuck my hand out. She didn't shake it.

"Mother, this has nothing to do with Camille. I chose to lie to you on my own because I knew you were gon' be trippin'," Walter said.

"*Gon' be trippin'?*" his mother mocked. "Do you think they talk like that at Princeton? Do you think you can have a career in politics talking like that? Not only that, you have a very important exam tomorrow, and you're up here hanging out! You *gon' be* at the community college if you keep this up!"

Walter rolled his eyes. His mother turned her attention back to me. I was still standing there, not sure what to say. "Is this what he turns into, hanging around you? A lying, Ebonics-talking—"

"Stop it, Mother!" Walter said. He was trying to keep his voice down, even though the people at the table next to us had already begun to stare.

I gave her a funny look, not quite sure what she meant by her little comment. She ignored me.

"Walter, I am so disappointed in you. Let's go," she said.

Walter blew a frustrated breath, then stared at his mother before sitting back down. "I'll be home when I'm finished."

His mother's mouth dropped open. "Wha—"

Walter snapped his head toward his mother. "I said, I'll be home when I'm finished!"

His mother looked like she was about to go off, but then she looked around at the people who had started to stare, and she must've decided against it. "We will finish this conversation at home. I expect you there by ten o'clock!" she said.

With that, she turned and stormed out of the restaurant.

I eased back into my seat. "Why didn't you tell me you had an exam?"

"It's just the S.A.T. I've already taken it and aced it, but my mother wants me to take it again to score even higher so that I can qualify for this prestigious award she wants me to have." He lowered his head and began toying with his napkin. "I just want to be an ordinary guy. Not some superstar senator's son."

I took his hand and squeezed it. I felt bad for him. Shoot, I felt bad for us, because I couldn't help but feel like there was no way I'd ever get his mother to like me.

8

Alexis

I don't believe you spent fifteen thousand dollars!" My father's voice roared through the house.

I immediately jumped up and turned up the volume on the stereo system me and the girls were listening to. We all had been practicing interviewing each other. Now we were just lounging around my family room, listening to music.

Although I tried to focus on my friends, I couldn't help but think about my parents fighting—again. That they had to choose this particular time to fight only made me even angrier. They knew I had company.

"Since when did I have to check with you before I spend money? It's my money, too!" my mother shouted.

Why did it sound like they were in the same room with me? We were in the downstairs family room. My parents were in my father's office, right next door. Still, you'd think in this big ol' house you wouldn't be able to hear through the walls like this.

"Fifteen thousand dollars? I can't believe you think it's okay to spend five grand on a few measly outfits. This makes no sense," I heard my father shout.

I couldn't turn the music up any higher without my friends knowing exactly what I was trying to do. It would be way too obvious, not to mention even more embarrassing. Besides, I know my friends heard them already. Heck, the whole neighborhood heard them.

"What makes no sense is this conversation. When you wanted a new motorcycle, I didn't start screaming because you went out and spent money on a bike that you've conveniently lost interest in. Now you want to try and itemize the things that I buy. Necessary things," my mother yelled. My mother was always yelling at my father.

I heard a crashing noise, then my father's voice. "Necessary? How exactly does pairs of Manolo Blaniks for seventeen hundred dollars each keep our family together?" my father screamed. "Then there's the day at the spa for twenty-three hundred dollars? What exactly did they do to you there? You spend money like I make it in the backyard or something!"

"These are things that make me feel good about myself," my mother responded.

I rolled my eyes toward the wall. I wished I was anywhere but home, stuck in the middle of a sleepover gone terribly wrong, listening to the latest of my parents' many fights. This time it was about money. Last time it was a fight over renovating the family room. The time before that it was about our family vacation. It was always something. I was so sick of the constant arguing and bickering that my parents had been doing. But for them to be arguing when they knew doggone well that I was having friends over, well, that was just too much. They had finally crossed the line this time.

I wanted to go knock on the door and give them a piece of my mind, but I knew all that would do was end the fight for now. Then, once me and my friends were close to falling asleep, they'd start right back up. I just wanted to vanish into thin air, especially when Jasmine looked at me and said, "Are your parents gonna be okay?"

Camille and Angel looked at each other funny, then they looked at me like they felt all sorry for me.

That's when I knew I couldn't take it anymore. Without answering Jasmine's question, I reached up and used my fist to bang on the wall. "Would y'all cut it out!" I screamed.

There was immediate silence. I envisioned the look on my parents' faces. But I was just grateful that the bickering had stopped.

"Yeah, they can get stupid sometimes. Let's just try and ignore 'em," I suggested.

Angel grabbed a fistful of popcorn and started stuffing her mouth as Camille and Jasmine jumped up and started dancing to the new Omarion song. We were interrupted a few minutes later by the sound of the doorbell ringing several times.

I jumped up and headed to the door. My mother almost knocked me down as she rushed past me. She flew across the marble-floored foyer and swung the front door wide open.

"I'm so glad you guys are here. He's right in the office," my mother sobbed as she pointed toward my father's office.

I thought I was going to die as I watched one police officer come into our home and the other stand at the door, trying to calm my mother down.

"Are you okay?" he asked.

"No, I'm not," my mother snapped.

"Did he hit you?" the officer asked.

"No, of course he didn't. I just called you all to make him get out," my mother cried.

The officer sighed, then motioned for my mother to have a seat on the living room sofa.

"Wow. Your mother called the cops on your dad?" Camille whispered. I didn't even realize she and the other girls had come up behind me.

I was too outdone. My parents had never embarrassed me as much as they had that very moment.

The cops didn't arrest my father, but they did ask him to leave. Right after they left, my mother locked herself in her bedroom. I told everyone to move upstairs to my bedroom, where I plopped down on my bed, grabbed a pillow, and pulled it close to my chest. "I'm so sorry, guys. I don't know why my parents flipped out like that," I said.

"I just can't believe the cops made your dad leave," Jasmine said.

I shook my head and sighed. "He probably left on his own. I'm sure he's gonna go get a room somewhere until she calms down. I told you guys my mother is nothing but a drama queen. Y'all don't see how she flips out sometimes, especially on my dad. I feel sorry for him. Actually, I feel sorry for her, too. Every since we put my sister away, my mother has turned into someone I don't know."

I felt myself tearing up as I thought about Sharon. She was in a place called Memorial Greens, which specializes in autistic children. Sharon was four years older than me, and it had crushed my mother to have to put her in that place ten years ago, but the family just couldn't handle her anymore. I think my mom blamed herself for Sharon being the way she was. In fact, when we put Sharon in that hospital is when everything just seemed to go downhill for my family. The sad part was, we didn't even go visit her that much. My mother said it was too depressing, and my father was always too busy.

Camille got up from the chair and came over to where I was sitting.

"I had no idea," Camille said. "I guess I just thought your life was perfect, or at least very close to being perfect. I mean, you guys are obviously rich, and your mom seems so cool."

"I kept trying to tell you guys things aren't all hunky-dory over here. My family has some serious issues. My parents argue so much, it's wild. Sometimes I really think they're gonna get a divorce. I swear I'm never ever getting married." I didn't mean to sound like some whiny child, but I was really upset.

"Girl, please," Jasmine said, socking my arm playfully. "Just because they act like that doesn't mean you and your husband are gon' do the same. Besides, you should be glad you even have your dad in your life."

I know she was thinking about her father, who she had just met a few months ago. Their little reunion didn't go as planned, and she'd been pretty bummed out about it.

"It's not my dad I have problems with," I said, snapping back to my conversation. "It's my mom and all her mess. I mean, my dad gets on my nerves too, but, uuggghhh, my mom, she's just too much."

I knew all of them also had issues with their mothers. But I don't think their problems could even begin to compare to mine. My family was falling apart, and I was caught right dead in the middle.

9

Alexis

I had so much fun last night. After I got over my parents' fighting, we'd had a really good time. I hated to see everyone leave this morning, but Camille and Jasmine had to go to church. I had planned to be right behind them, heading somewhere, until the housekeeper came and told me my mother wanted to see me. Of course, I had no desire to see her, since I was still mad about the way my parents acted in front of my friends.

I looked up at the spiral staircase and rolled my eyes at the thought of having to face my mother. I finally pulled myself up the stairs and walked toward my parents' bedroom.

I knocked on the door softly and prayed my mother had fallen back to sleep.

"C'mon in," my mother said.

When I opened the door and looked around, I noticed my mother on the bed, surrounded by a mountain of fluffy pillows. She wore a pair of silk pajamas that matched the champagne-colored down comforter, and a sleep mask was pulled up onto her forehead.

"Oh, darling." My mother used her hand to pat a space next to her on the bed. "Come and let's talk. I'm so sorry about last night. It's just your daddy can be so impossible at times."

I didn't feel like I had any choice, so I scooted up onto the bed next to her.

"I can't believe you called the police on him, Mama. How could you do that?" I knew nothing my mother said could justify what she did, but I needed some type of explanation of how she could do something so horrible.

"I called them because your father wouldn't leave like I told him to."

"But it's his house, too, Mama."

"Well, regardless, the cops didn't even have to put him out, honey. He volunteered to leave. And you know what, I'm glad he did. I just can't take this stress right now. I think the time apart may do us some good." She touched my hand. "But I just want you to know that our arguments have nothing to do with you. And I really don't want you to worry about them."

Not worry? How could I not worry? They sounded like they were about to kill each other.

"Sometimes I feel like your father just doesn't understand me," my mother continued. "For him everything is about the next big acquisition, the next real estate deal. He doesn't understand the pressure I'm under."

I couldn't believe my mother was sitting here talking about pressure, like she actually had a care in the world. She didn't work. Her days were filled with hair, nails, and spa appointments. Then there was the shopping. My mother didn't shop like normal people. No, she visited celebrity designers, and had to have top-of-the-line everything.

"I try to tell your father, pumpkin, that home is just as important as work. I mean, what does he expect his girls to do while he travels the country day after day?" She sighed. In a dramatic fashion that I was used to seeing, she draped her hand over her sleep mask and eased back onto the pillows.

"Do you know he made me go to a charity event unescorted last week?" She gasped. "It's like my social events aren't even important to him. But I'm expected to be the good wife when he needs someone at his side." My mother is such a drama queen.

"Oh, honey, I don't mean to trouble you with all of this," she continued. "It's just sometimes men can be so disagreeable." She shook her head before forcing a smile. "Did Sonja leave any of that bacon I smelled earlier?"

"No, Mom, we ate it all," I said.

"We?" she asked with a puzzled look on her face.

"Did you forget that I was having a sleepover last night? The girls just left," I said. Why did it not surprise me that my mother didn't remember my sleepover? It seemed nothing I did was a priority in her or my dad's life.

"Oh, darling, I'm so sorry your little friends had to witness that," she said.

"It's no big deal," I lied.

"No big deal?" She sighed heavily. "No big deal? Sweetie, I'm so sorry. Your father, the way he behaves sometimes is just baffling. You and your father both know how emotional I can get sometimes. So for him to overreact the way he did, well, it's just a shame is what it is."

I shook my head. "It really is no big deal."

Part of me wanted to go off, but the other part was just sick as I listened to my mom go on and on about how she is the real victim here.

"Pumpkin, I was thinking maybe we should have a sweetheart's day. We could go to the spa, have facials, get our hair and nails done and have lunch at the country club. Then we could go have dinner anywhere you like." She smiled.

I did not want to hang out with her, much less be seen with her, after that stunt she pulled last night.

"I can't. Me and Jaquan are going to go catch a movie." The words were out of my mouth before I knew it. I wasn't ready to tell my mother about Jaquan yet. But it was too late. She sat up.

"Jaquan? Who is that?"

"My boyfriend." I let out a deep breath. Jaquan and I had just started going together last week, after he asked me over the phone to be his girlfriend. I was so excited and wanted to tell Angel and Camille, but I didn't want to say anything to them until I had a chance to talk to Jasmine first. And I just couldn't bring myself to do it last night.

Regardless, I was kicking myself now. My mom was so nosy and I didn't want to give her a whole bunch of details.

"Since when did you get a boyfriend and not tell your mother about it?"

I rolled my eyes.

"So, tell me," she said excitedly when I didn't answer, "is he from a good family? What do his parents do for a living? Where is he from? Oh, this is so special. My baby has a boyfriend."

I sighed. "He's Jasmine's brother, ma."

With the look on my mother's face, you would have thought I told her I was dating Shrek or something.

"Jasmine, as in your little ghetto friend Jasmine?"

"Jasmine is not ghetto," I protested.

"Jasmine who lives in public housing Jasmine?"

"Mama, please," I said. She made me so sick. "Jaquan is cool, and I like him a lot."

My mother got up and started pacing the floor. "Lexi, sweetheart, you know I think Jasmine is a sweet girl, and I'm sure her brother is a really nice guy. But you're meant to be with a certain type of boy."

I looked at my mother, wondering how in the world she got to be such a snob.

"What type, Mom? Someone with money?"

My mother didn't catch my sarcasm. "That's always good." She exhaled deeply. "Look, I don't want to argue with you after the night I had with your father. I do not want you to see that boy. And that's final. Do you understand?"

"No, I don't understand!"

"All those boys at the country club, or even at your school, and you want to go hook up with some thug from across town." My mother shook her head. "Sometimes I just don't understand you, Lexi. I don't want you to see that boy, and it's not open for discussion." She slapped her legs. "Now, as I was saying earlier, let's do a day at the spa."

My mother didn't give me time to respond before she jumped up and began punching numbers into the phone.

"Yes, this is Veronique Lansing. I want an appointment for my daughter and myself for later this afternoon." She flashed me a smile. I rolled my eyes.

She quickly made an appointment, then hung up the phone. "We're going to have so much fun. Now you run and get dressed so that we can start on our special day."

"I am dressed," I snapped. I was praying this wasn't one of those times when she'd want us to either dress alike or wear the same colors. I hated when my parents fought, not just because it was embarrassing, loud, and worked my nerves, but after the infamous fights, my mom felt like she had go out for the Mother of the Year awards. And that usually left me stuck in the middle of the makeup war, too.

See, Dad picks up on what she's doing, then next thing you know I'm off to the golf course or some other place I don't wanna go. When my parents fight, I'm the one who really suffers.

Mom's eyes roamed up and down my fringed-edged lowrider jeans and my "I Like Cute Boys" tank top. She turned up her nose.

"This is an exclusive spa, darling. Why don't you wear that sweater twin set and that black skirt I like," she said, prancing over to her massive walk-in closet.

"But I'm comfortable," I said.

"Yes, I know. But you can't step into this place looking like we don't belong. Now run and get ready, dear." She was deep in the closet before I could say anything else.

I dragged myself back to my bedroom to change. After I'd changed out of my jeans, I laid across my bed and began absentmindedly flipping through the channels. When I heard a knock on my bedroom door a few minutes later, I thought about not answering. But then I figured she'd barge her way in if I didn't, so I got up, opened the door, and tried not to let my frustration show.

Mom's eyes got big and her mouth fell open as she looked at me. She started shaking her head and stormed right over to my closet.

"I did not tell you to change out of those horrid jeans just so you could put on some warm-ups," she snapped.

I pouted, plopped down on the bed, and crossed my arms across my chest.

It didn't take long for Mom to come walking out of the closet clutching the sweater twin set and skirt she first told me to put on.

"The car is waiting, so you need to hurry and change. We have a full day ahead," she said before turning and rushing toward my bedroom door.

"Does it matter that I don't want to go?" I sat up, my arms still folded.

She spun around and looked at me with beady eyes. "I'm not in the mood today, Lexi. Now get dressed and meet me downstairs. I'll be waiting in the car."

I sighed in frustration. Just once, I wish someone would care what I want. Thank God for Jaquan. He was the only bright spot in my life. And I didn't care what my mother said, we were going to be together forever.

10

Camille

$\mathcal{I}$ watched as Jasmine stared at the big red letter scratched across the top of her exam. I leaned over to her desk and looked at it.

"F?" I asked.

She held the test toward me and whispered. "A big F. How in the world did I get an F?"

I couldn't help but smile when she said that. "Ummm, let's see. Didn't you say you started studying the morning of the test? You know Mrs. Reed is hard, and you can't do any last-minute studying for her class."

Jasmine let out a groan. "Shut up. What did you get?"

I held up my paper. "A-minus." I was just about to gloat some more, but the way she slumped back in her seat made me change my mind. I know Jasmine had been bummed out ever since she and Donovan broke up last week. But I tried to tell her. I don't know how she thought she was gon' hang on to that boy when he went off to college, especially since she still hadn't had sex with him. I mean, he was playing basketball at the University of Texas at Austin, and he was fine as all get-out. I just knew those college girls would be all over him. Jasmine didn't stand a chance.

"Are you okay?" I asked, just as the bell rang.

Jasmine gathered her books. "I'm straight."

We both stood up and started heading toward the door. I knew I probably shouldn't go there, but I was curious, so I asked, "You heard from Donovan?"

She stopped right outside the classroom door. Her eyes got sad at the mention of his name. "Nah, I tried to call him yesterday but his roommate was talking about he wasn't there. I know he was lying. I heard some girls giggling in the background."

"I'm sorry."

Jasmine shrugged. "Don't be. I'll be fine. Forget Donovan."

I was just about to say something else when Tameka came bouncing toward us. "What's up?"

"What's up with you?" I said. Tameka actually had opened up a little at our last meeting. We'd even laughed a few times. Now she was bouncing around, all happy. Maybe she'd gotten out of the funk she'd been in the first few weeks she joined the Good Girlz.

"Hey," Jasmine echoed.

"Y'all ready for the audition?" Tameka asked.

"You know I am," Camille said.

"Shoot, I forgot all about the audition," Jasmine responded.

"How you gon' forget?" Tameka asked.

"I had a lot on my mind."

"Well, I have the tape from our practice run right here," Tameka said as she waved a VHS tape back and forth. She'd made the tape of us practicing at our meeting Tuesday night, saying it would help us all to be able to critique ourselves. She'd called her cousin for tips on how we could interview each other and then videotaped us as we practiced.

"I would've waited and brought it to the meeting Thursday, but you know we gotta meet the girls we're supposed to be mentoring," Tameka continued. "Besides, I don't know about you, but I don't want to wait. I already talked with Mr. White in the TV department. He said we can use the studio to review the tape."

"Cool," I said. Since our school was a magnet school for communications, we had a state-of-the-art television studio where students could get hands-on experience in the television and radio business. "When can we watch it?" I asked. I was really geeked about the auditions. Not just for the money, but because hosting the show would have been so much fun. So I wanted to make sure I gave it my all, and I was anxious to see how the practice run went.

"After school. Just meet me in the TV studios," Tameka said as she raced down the hall to class. "I have Mrs. Reed now, so I can't be late. I'll see you all after school."

We waved to Tameka. "Maybe she wasn't so bad after all," I mumbled to Jasmine as we headed to our next classes.

Jasmine shot me a "yeah, right" look before heading to her class.

I met Alexis after school outside the gate, then walked her back to the studios. I had sent her a text message to meet us after school. She had a free sixth period, so she was waiting by the time our dismissal bell rang.

When we walked into the studio, Jasmine, Angel, and Tameka were already there.

"Hey, everybody," Alexis said as she walked in.

Everybody waved as Tameka popped the tape in. "I watched the tape last night, so I have a few critiques myself," she said.

We all looked at Tameka like, Who died and appointed her audition queen?

First up on the tape was me interviewing Angel. I smiled as I watched myself give a brief introduction, then welcome Angel to the show. Part of our audition included interviewing another person about a hot teen topic. So that's what we were practicing when we taped the fake interviews. Angel looked so cute and innocent as she talked about cheating on tests.

"Okay." Tameka stood up, paused the tape, then turned to me. "Camille, you see how you're leaning in. You need to be aware of that, because it's distracting. And Angel, you're not making eye contact."

Me and Angel looked at her like she was crazy, but we didn't say anything.

Tameka pushed play again, and we watched a few more minutes of the tape before she stopped it again. "Okay, Camille, you're going to have to have a little more personality."

Jasmine spoke up before I could respond. "Excuse me," she said, waving her hand. "Since when did you become the talk show expert? I'm just wondering, because I must've missed the memo or something."

Tameka folded her arms and cut her eyes. "I'm trying to help you all out. I'm the only one here who has some television training."

"You sat in the audience at one taping of the Nickelodeon awards. That hardly qualifies as training," Alexis said. Tameka had let it be known about her Nickelodeon experience. The way she boasted, you would have thought she starred with Nick Cannon in a Nick Movie of the Week.

"It's more than you've done," Tameka said defensively. "Besides, my cousin—"

"Yeah, yeah," I cut her off. "We know, your cousin is a reporter for CNN."

"Whatever." Tameka threw her arms up. "Y'all can look crazy all you want, then. But don't be mad when I win this competition hands-down."

"I thought we agreed that you guys wouldn't see this as a competition," Angel said.

"Well, I wasn't, which is why I was trying to go through the tape with y'all," Tameka said. "I mean, if you want to know the truth, I'm the only one who even stands a chance."

Okay, this girl was smoking something for real. I stood up because I saw Jasmine getting worked up.

"Look, Tameka," I said. "I'm sure you think you have what it takes to win this thing. Heck, we all do. But one thing we agreed on was that we would keep this a friendly competition."

Tameka rolled her eyes and leaned back in to the TV. She pushed eject on the tape. "That's what I was trying to do." She pulled the tape out. "But obviously you all don't appreciate that."

"Tameka, chill out," Alexis said. "Nobody's upset with you trying to help. I think it's just the way you came across."

Tameka stuffed the tape in her backpack, then slung the backpack over her shoulder. "Well, you know what? You don't have to worry about how I come across anymore, because I'm out." She turned and stomped out the door.

We all sighed in frustration. So much for thinking she'd changed.

Camille

$\mathcal{W}$alter and I sat in the parking lot of the Channel 2 studios. I was nervous as all get-out, but he was trying his best to calm me down. He was dropping me off for the on-air test with the producers.

"I told you, you got this," he said, stroking my hair.

"I'm just worried I'm going to freeze up," I replied.

"Please. This is what you want to do when you grow up, so you'll do fine."

His calmness and confidence eased my fears. I smiled.

"Now, you need to get going." He pointed to the digital clock on his dashboard. "To be early is to be on time. To be on time is to be late."

"Okay, now you sound like Mrs. Reed, my history teacher." I laughed as I gathered up my purse and backpack. Today was the day the producers saw what we looked like on camera and decided if we'd even take this audition any further.

"You know I wish I could go inside with you," he said.

"Yeah, right. I'm nervous enough. I would sho' mess up if you were in there with me."

He grinned. "Call me as soon as it's over."

I gave him a quick kiss and made my way inside.

I was in awe at the huge lobby. All of the anchors' pictures were lined up against the wall. I recognized two of my favorites, Melinda Spaulding and Damali Keith. I remember I used to imitate them, dreaming of the day I could take their places. And to think, I could actually be working in the same building as them.

I checked in with the receptionist, who led me down a long hallway into the TV studio, which was freezing cold.

Alexis, Jasmine, Tameka, and Angel were already inside, seated in chairs next to a huge news desk. I immediately recognized this as the place they taped the news every day.

I spoke to everyone. They all looked just as nervous as me. Even Angel looked nervous, and she wasn't even auditioning.

"You ready?" Alexis whispered as I sat down.

I shook my head from side to side. She laughed. "Me neither."

We didn't have time to talk, as Shereen and five other people came in.

"Hello, ladies," Shereen said as she walked to the front of the room. "You ready to do this?"

We all smiled and nodded our heads.

She clapped her hands together. "Well, good. This is Bernadette, LaShauna, LaQuanta, and Dana," she said, pointing to four of the people on her right side. "They are the producers for the show, and they'll be judging your on-air test. This"—she pointed to the fifth person—"is our intern, Danielle. She will be helping us out today." Shereen turned to a stage, which was sitting under some huge lights. "Now, this is our set. We have actually decided to combine your interview with the on-air test. So you'll be answering your questions on camera." She looked at us and smiled. "Let's get started." She glanced at her clipboard. "Camille, you're first. Followed by Jasmine, then Alexis, then Tameka."

Shereen took her seat behind a big TV screen sitting on a table. Three of the other producers sat at a big table. The producer named Bernadette sat in one of the chairs on the set.

"Sit down. I don't bite," Bernadette said with a laugh.

Dang. I wanted to kick myself. I didn't want to appear nervous. I tried to smile as I walked over and sat down next to her.

Bernadette didn't give me time to relax; she just jumped right into the interview.

"So tell me, Camille, why do you think you have what it takes to be our new host?" she said.

Why did I have to be first? "Well, ummm, I'm what you

guys are looking for." I went on to talk about all the quali-
ties I would bring to the job. The interview lasted about
ten minutes. I actually got better as it went on. The first
few minutes were rough, though, with me stumbling all
over the place. But after that, I think I did all right.

After I was done, Bernadette thanked me and quickly
shuffled Jasmine up. I couldn't judge what she thought by
the look on her face. Shoot, all the producers had these
blank looks. That was really frustrating.

Jasmine's interview was okay. Honestly, she's my girl
and all, but she looked uncomfortable sitting up on the
stage. She kept gaping her legs open—I guess it was a hard
habit to break from her tomboy days.

Alexis did pretty well. She seemed a lot more relaxed
than both of us.

By the time they got to Tameka, I wondered whether
the producers were getting tired, because I saw Dana yawn
and stretch.

Bernadette pretty much went through the same spiel
with Tameka. I watched in awe as Tameka worked her
jelly. She made jokes, looked at the camera, and even had
Bernadette laughing.

"Bernadette, I know we're just about out of time,"
Tameka said, sounding all natural, "but I just have to say,
if you're looking for a teen who's in touch with the happenings in the community, who has what it takes to make *Teen
Talks* one of the more talked-about shows in town, that

would be me." She reached out and shook Bernadette's hand. "And I'd be honored to be your host."

Why hadn't I thought to make a last-minute pitch for the job?

"Thank you, Tameka," Bernadette said, obviously pleasantly surprised.

"No, thank you, Bernadette." Tameka turned toward the camera and flashed a smile. "And thank you, Dana, LaQuanta, LaShauna, and Shereen, for giving me this opportunity."

How the heck did she remember everyone's names?

"This is your girl Tameka for *Teen Talks*. Until next week, see you out and about, because we're all over town, gathering up the latest, hippest happenings to bring your way! Peace." She flashed two fingers and smiled.

I looked at Alexis, Jasmine, and Angel. Like me, their mouths were hanging open. Even the dang producers were smiling. I think all of us were shocked at how well Tameka had done.

"Can you believe that?" Jasmine whispered.

Too stunned to talk, I watched as Tameka walked off the stage with an air of confidence I'd never seen before. She came and took her seat back next to us and looked at us as if to say, "Take that."

"Well," Shereen said as she made her way to the front. "You ladies did great. I definitely think we've found our host among you all."

Tameka stuck her chest out as she raised her hand. "Miss Young, will you all let us know how we did?"

Shereen looked at the other producers and chuckled. "I guess you want to know if you were as good as you think you were?"

Tameka looked like she didn't know how to take that. Her smile started fading, but Shereen quickly made it pop back.

"You were." Shereen turned back to us. "All of you were, actually. But we'll be in touch through Rachel and let you know where we go from here, all right?"

Me, Alexis, and Jasmine nodded as we slowly got up to follow the intern out. Was my dream of hosting the show over as fast as it had begun? Of all people to lose to, why did it have to be Tameka?

"Oh," Shereen interrupted, "please let me add that this is still anyone's show to win. No matter how well you did or didn't do today, remember, the audition process is not over."

That made me feel better. Maybe I still had a shot.

"Girl, you were off the chain," the intern said to Tameka as she walked us back to the front. She and Tameka were walking a few steps in front of us. "Have you done TV before?"

Tameka smiled. "I've been on Nickelodeon, and my cousin is a reporter at CNN."

"Oh, that must be it, because you definitely seem like a natural pro," the girl said.

Me, Alexis, Jasmine, and Angel all looked at one another and rolled our eyes.

The intern turned back to us. "I mean, you guys did good, too," she threw in before turning back to Tameka. "But girl, you got this TV thing down. I wish I was as good as you."

I shook my head. Why was that girl filling Tameka's head?

After today, I just knew Tameka and her attitude were only going to go from bad to worse.

12

Camille

*M*y heartbeat was thumping so loud as I leaned up against the stairwell, trying to make sure they didn't see me. I couldn't believe my ears. My mother was listening to this crap like this woman actually had a point. Why didn't she stop this woman's crazy talk?

"So, I think Camille is a really, really sweet girl. I love what you've done with her. She's so articulate, and she carries herself just like a little young lady."

I waited for my mother to go off or say something to show that she was just a little bit offended by what this woman was saying. But nothing happened. I peeked around the corner to see if maybe my mother had used some kind of silent technique to drop-kick her without me knowing. Of course she hadn't.

They stood at the front door, inches from each other. I wanted to jump from my hiding spot up against the stairs and confront Walter's mom myself, but it was obvious that being quiet and out of sight would be my better option.

My mother was just coming in from her first job when Mrs. Lewis popped up. She hadn't even made it in the door good when she looked up to find this strange woman standing there, smiling. Mrs. Lewis had called my mom for some reason earlier this week, but my mom wouldn't go into details about what she wanted. But I'm sure she didn't know Mrs. Lewis would be showing up on her doorstep today. She even had the nerve to be holding a basket filled with what looked like chocolate chip cookies. I couldn't believe it. My mother didn't know I was home because I was supposed to be at the church, helping Rachel with some stuff, but we wrapped up early. My plan was to run home and change real quick so that Walter and I could sneak out together.

I hid behind the stairs when I heard the keys rattling at the front door. I stepped back a few feet, and listened.

"Hi there, you must be Lydia, Camille's mom," Mrs. Lewis said. "I'm so glad I caught you. I really was just taking a chance by showing up here," she said. I saw her look around as if she was concerned for her safety. Walter's mom had her golden blond hair pinned up in a French bun. Her skin was perfectly tanned. And even from where I stood, peeking around the corner, I could see the large diamonds that sparkled from her ears to her neck to her thin fingers.

"I am Lydia, and you are?" my mother asked curtly.

"Oh, I'm sorry. I'm Penelope, Walter's mom. Remember we talked on the phone the other day, and I told you then that I'd like to meet for a few minutes?"

My mother let out a fake laugh, the one she used when she really didn't know what to say. I'm sure she probably wanted to tell Mrs. Lewis she had only thirty minutes to change, fix a lunch, and rush out to make it to her next job on time. I knew exactly what she was thinking because I watched as she sighed, then stepped back a bit. Mrs. Lewis didn't even really step all the way inside the house, so they stood in the doorway with the door wide open.

"I didn't realize you meant this soon, and without even calling," my mother said.

"Oh, yes, I'm so sorry about that. But really it was just an impulse that brought me over here. I had business nearby, and well, I was just hoping you had some time. This is really important," she said.

My mother flicked her wrist to check her watch, then she said, "I've got a few minutes. I take it this is about the problem we discussed right?"

Mrs. Lewis nodded. She looked around, then said, "You mind if I come in?"

"Oh, where's my manners?" My mother sighed and stepped aside. "Please, come in. Would you like a seat?"

Mrs. Lewis glanced around again, the look on her face saying she didn't trust sitting on our tattered furniture. She looked like a fish out of water. I pulled my head back when she walked farther into the house.

"I won't take up much of your time. I just wanted to make sure that you and I are on the same page. I know as a mother you want what's best for your child, as I do for mine." Walter's mom shook her head like she was just about to deliver devastating news.

"And my Walter is such a super kid," she continued. "His father and I are so very lucky. We know we've done a terrific job with him. Did you know he has already been accepted at Princeton?"

Before my mother could even answer, Mrs. Lewis continued. "Well, we just think, his father and I believe, that this is really a crucial time for our son. And as parents, well, it's our responsibility to do what we feel is best for him. And we, well, we just don't think him getting involved in a serious relationship at this time is the right thing to do. We just don't think he needs that kind of distraction right now. I'm sure you understand just what I'm saying."

When my mother cleared her throat and shifted her weight to one side, I just knew Mrs. Lewis was about to get it.

"Oh, these," Mrs. Lewis said nervously as she looked down at the cookies. "I brought these for you." She shoved the basket at my mother in a way that forced her to accept it. My mother looked down at the cookies, did her fake smile, and placed the basket on the coffee table.

"Thanks," she said. "But I've been thinking about what you said, and I think you should know—" Mrs. Lewis held up her index finger as her cell phone rang, cutting off my mother while she reached in her purse to get it.

I watched them as Mrs. Lewis answered. She paused, then threw her head back and released a phony laugh.

"Well, Vivian, darling, let me just say this. If you are going to wear that gown, we'll all have to start working out this very second. Everyone knows how fabulous your figure is, and that design will just be the icing on the cake. You're sure to outshine us all. But look, sweetie, I'm right in the middle of something awfully important right now, so do you mind if I get back to you in a bit?"

There was silence.

"Yes, I promise, the minute I wrap this up. Smooches, darling." She snapped the phone shut and looked at my mother after tucking the phone back into her purse. "I apologize for that. My friend and I have this debutante event coming up, and we're just a wreck about what to wear. Don't you hate that?" she asked. She didn't wait for an answer before she leaned in close to my mom, like they were old friends. "It's actually her daughter's coming-out event, and as quiet as it's kept, since Walter and Valencia were babies, we've always dreamed of them attending together. Now Walter is saying he doesn't even want to go."

Mrs. Lewis placed her hand across her chest as if she were really hurting. "Imagine the nightmare that's causing.

So you can see what confusion this thing with your daughter has caused. I'm sure you understand my concern. And, well"—she shrugged—"I just really hope I can get your help with this situation."

"So let me get this straight," my mother said.

Now that's what I'm talking about. I knew once she got my mother going, it'd be on for real. My mom is pretty laid-back until someone messes with her baby—me.

"It sounds to me like you think your son is too good for my daughter," my mother snapped.

Yeah, that's right. Get her, Mama.

Mrs. Lewis threw her hands up in surrender and actually stepped back a few feet. Her little green eyes widened in horror.

"I'll have you know, I have black friends," she quickly defended. "We donate to all of those little orphanages in Africa! Well, maybe not all of them, but you know what I mean." By now, her face had turned a shade or two of red. Veins were popping at her temple and her neck. She was pointing her own finger at her chest. "No one can accuse my family of being racist! You don't know anything about me." Her lips were trembling.

"Look, I don't have to know you to know I don't appreciate you coming into my house acting like you're tossing compliments around when you're not doing a doggone thing but stirring up trouble," my mother said. "And FYI—I never said a thing about color."

That's right, Mama. I was so proud of her at that very moment, I wanted to jump in and cosign with a few comments of my own. But the next words to fall from my mother's lips quickly wiped away my smile.

"But since we're on the topic, do you think I want my daughter bouncing around with that son of yours? I know what people like you think when you see an interracial couple. I don't want my daughter to have to suffer through that. I don't want them together any more than you do, but you're not about to come up in my house trying to play some reverse psychology on me. You tell your little perfect Princeton-bound son to stop sniffin' around my daughter, and maybe you won't have to lower yourself to such unpleasant work," my mother said.

Needless to say, all of the triumph I felt only moments ago was gone. I wanted her to defend my relationship with Walter, not tear it down. I wanted her to put his mother in her place, not find a way to agree with her. My heart sank when Mrs. Lewis turned around and stormed out of the front door in a huff.

I slid down against the wall and wrapped my arms around my legs. I no longer cared if my mother realized I was home.

I heard her slam the front door, mumble a few choice words, and rush into the kitchen. While she moved around in there, I was burning with fury. I started to go in there and confront her myself, but I was too upset. Besides, I may have been mad, but I wasn't crazy. After a few minutes, I looked up. My mother had come around the corner and stood right there in front of me.

"How long have you been sitting here?" she asked, a frown plastered across her face.

"Long enough to hear." I couldn't bring myself to look at her.

"You have to understand, I just want what's best," my mother said.

"Best for who?"

I glared at my mother. She didn't respond at first. Finally she said, "Camille, seeing that boy is just opening the door for problems. Now, if you don't listen to anything else I say, listen to this. Stay away from that boy and his family."

There was nothing I could say. I didn't care what Mrs. Lewis thought. I didn't care what my mom said. I didn't care what anyone said. There was no way in the world I was going to stay away from Walter.

13

Alexis

It had been a long day, and I wasn't in a good mood. My parents had been fighting all day. I heard them arguing when I left for school this morning, and they were still at it when I came home. I'd locked myself in my room and tried to turn up my TV to drown out the fighting.

Finally I'd gotten sick of listening to it and left to go hang out with Jaquan, but neither he nor Jasmine were at home. I felt myself falling hard for Jaquan, but I did wish we spent more time together. He was just always with his boys, although we had gone to the movies last night.

Since I couldn't catch up with him or Jasmine, I went to hang out at the mall until tonight's Good Girlz meeting. I charged up a few things. Well, not really a few. Almost six hundred dollars worth of stuff that I didn't even need. I had just signed the sales slip when the young saleslady handed me my bags.

"Must be nice to shop like that," she said.

I forced a smile. "It's all compliments of my dad."

She laughed. "Wow. Well, get ready to get it when he sees that bill. He's probably gon' hit the roof."

"I don't think so," I said, wondering why she was all up in my business.

I took my bags and left the store as her words danced in my head. My father hit the roof about something I did? Fat chance of that happening. He would probably just pay the bill without even questioning me about it. Now, he loses it when my mother spends money. But me, he doesn't say a word. I think it's because he feels guilty about never being around. And probably because I never spend more than a few hundred dollars. My mom, on the other hand? It's nothing for her to spend thousands and thousands of dollars.

I know it sounds crazy, but just once I'd love to get in trouble about something. I mean real trouble, like have my dad go off or scream or something. Heck, I'd even take a whipping. At least I'd know my parents cared. Don't get me wrong, I'm not stupid, but I've never in my life had a spanking. My mother has tapped my hand before, but that's about it. I've been punished a few times, but that usually means just being sent to my room and not being able to watch TV or something. I don't want any of those beatings Jasmine claims she gets, but I do want my parents to act like they care. When my father gets the credit card bill, he'll probably give me a two-minute lecture on his way out the door, about how I need to manage money better. My mother will spend another three minutes telling me how so many poor people in the world wish they had money like us, then they'll go back to doing what they're doing. And I'll be left alone in my little world again.

I arrived at the meeting still down in the dumps. I made small talk with everyone, but I think they could all tell something was wrong.

Rachel got the meeting started. "Anything anybody wants to talk about today?"

Everyone looked at one another. A few eyebrows went up, Angel and Camille shrugged, and Tameka started examining her fingernails.

"Well, um, I kinda want to say something about my parents," I softly said.

"What's going on?" Rachel asked.

The room got really quiet. All eyes were on me. I ran my fingers through my hair, then sighed. "I know I can't stand my mom at times, and my dad gets on my nerves, but I really think they're gonna get a divorce, and I just don't know what I'm gonna do."

"Oh, sweetie," Rachel said. "Sometimes adults argue and bicker and fight, but it doesn't mean they're going to divorce."

I was hoping she didn't start quoting Bible scriptures about marriage, because while my parents said they were Christians, I just didn't think they kept God in their marriage, as the minister at our church is always talking about.

"Why is my family so messed up?" I asked Rachel.

Rachel smiled. "Honey, if I had that answer, I'd put Dr. Phil out of business." She rubbed my hand. "But trust me when I tell you, just when you think your situation is bad, there's always someone who's worse off."

"No. My family took the function out of dysfunctional," I said.

"Have you all ever done counseling?" Rachel asked.

"Yeah, right," I said, looking at her like she was crazy. "First of all, you'd have to get my dad to show up. Then if he did, he would talk about how some nerdy therapist can't fix his problems. Then my mom would find some way to make it all about her. Thanks, but no thanks."

"I'm talking about spiritual counseling. Like from your pastor. Or even here. Rev. Adams is great with couples."

Since my parents hardly went to church anymore, at least together, I doubted very seriously they had tried spiritual counseling.

Rachel smiled at me. "Why don't you suggest it to them?"

"Yeah, okay," I said, still not believing she was serious.

"What do you have to lose?"

I guess she was right about that. "Fine. I'll ask them."

Rachel stood up and walked to the front of the room. "In the meantime, why don't we say a prayer. So many times people get caught up in their lives, and they forget that God is at the center of everything we do. And when we lose sight of that, it's like we're losing the glue that holds everything together."

I couldn't help but stare at Rachel. Is that why my family was so jacked up? As a little girl, I remember we used to pray together as a family. We never missed a Sunday, and my mother would even read us Bible stories. What had happened to that? I racked my brain, trying to figure out if that was when things started going downhill for us.

Rachel started softly praying, and I felt a tear drop as I thought of my parents. I was so desperate that I'd try anything—even prayer. I was just hoping that God was listening.

14

Alexis

I stood outside my door, hating to go home. My father had missed yet another play performance. I was starring in *Romeo and Juliet,* and I'd been practicing for weeks. I got a standing ovation, and everyone was there. Everyone except my parents, that is.

I stuck my key in the door, dreading going inside because I just knew I was going to see my mother somewhere sulking. My father would be gone. And it would be me and whatever Sonja fixed for dinner in front of the TV.

People were always talking about they wish they had my life. Shoot, if they only knew.

I was surprised to see my mother sitting on the sofa, my father standing up in front of her. I found myself hoping they had a valid excuse for missing my play. I was about to say something when I noticed that my mother's eyes were red.

"Hi, sweetheart," my mother said, trying to plaster on a

smile. "I am so sorry we missed your play. Your father got sort of caught up at work."

"Surprise, surprise," I purposely mumbled loudly as I dropped my purse on the end table. "What's going on?"

That's when my eyes made their way over to the foot of the stairs, where I noticed four black leather bags.

"Daddy, are you going on a business trip?" I asked, not quite sure about why he would be taking so many bags.

"Sweetie, have a seat," my father said, motioning to the sofa.

Whenever someone says "sweetie, have a seat," you know he is not about to give you some good news. Kinda like a guy going on the *Maury Povich Show* with his girlfriend who has a secret to tell him, then being surprised when Maury says, "You are not the father."

"Somebody wanna tell me what's going on?" I said, without sitting down.

My father sighed and looked at my mother. She scared me because she looked away, and I swear there were real tears in her eyes. Not those drama crocodile tears she could turn on and off. "It's your idea, so you tell her." My mother's voice was soft and dejected. There was no attitude, no dramatics, just pain.

I looked at my father. "Daddy, are you leaving us?"

My father took a deep breath. "Baby, I'm not leaving you." He reached out to touch me. I jerked away.

"You're leaving Mom? You're leaving this house?" I knew this was a possibility, but now that it was actually happening, I was about to lose my mind. "How can you do this to us?"

"Lexi, you are old enough to understand this." He glanced over at my mother. She still had her head turned away but I could see the tears trickling down her cheeks.

"Your mother and I are getting a divorce."

I looked around the room, waiting for Ashton Kutcher to jump out and tell me I was being punked or something. No way my father was standing here saying this to me. "A divorce? You're not even going to separate first? I mean, don't you have to separate first? Isn't that the law?" I felt myself getting hysterical. I know my family was jacked up, but we were still a family. Images of my father moving out, remarrying, starting a whole new life without us, flashed in my mind.

"Sweetheart, we're past the point of separation," my father said.

I looked at my mother. "Mama, tell him don't do this. I know y'all been fighting, but you don't want this, I know you don't."

"It's for the best," my mother whispered.

My father walked over toward his bags. "Don't worry about anything, Lexi. Both you and your mother will be well taken care of."

I rushed over to where he was. "I don't care about your

money. I have never cared about your money. Please, Daddy, don't do this."

"It's done," he said, picking up his smallest bag.

"What about till death do you part? What about the vows you made before God?" I knew I was grasping at straws, but I would try anything to get them to come to their senses.

That must've caught my parents off guard, because both of them were quiet.

"You made a promise to God. Until death do you part," I said, looking back and forth between them.

My father looked at me. He, too, had tears in his eyes. He reached out and caressed my face. "Lexi, I love you. But living here is killing me. God will understand."

He reached down, picked up the rest of his bags, and walked out the front door. I heard my mother let out a loud moan just as the door slammed. I collapsed to the floor in tears.

15

Camille

$\mathcal{W}$here have you been? And don't even try saying you were at Alexis's, because I called over there, and her mother said Alexis was asleep and that neither of them had seen you."

I was cold busted. I didn't know what to say, and I couldn't think of a different story fast enough. I had taken off my shoes and tried my best to be as quiet as possible when I snuck into the back door. I was walking slowly on my tiptoes with my wedges and my purse in my hands, then suddenly the lights flicked on, nearly blinding me. I stared at my mother sitting on the sofa, her arms folded across her chest and I knew I was as good as dead.

Fire was burning in my mother's eyes, and I knew this was no time to lie. But what else could I do? She knew I hadn't been with Alexis, which is where I said I'd be. I knew I should've said I was spending the night, but that was the excuse I used last time I snuck out to be with Walter. Me and Walter had actually gone to that drive-in he told me about. It was so much fun, but it was near San Antonio, which was about two hours away. We had planned to be back by midnight, but everyone was hanging out afterward. Now it was almost two thirty in the morning.

"Well, young lady?" My mother's hands flew to her hips, as she stood up. She tapped one foot as she stood in front of me in her old tattered housecoat and rollers.

"First off, you're two hours past your curfew, and you come trying to sneak in here after you've been God knows where, and not to mention with who. I want answers, and I want them now!" she demanded.

I thought I was gon' pass out. I was so nervous I couldn't think of a lie fast enough.

"Camille? Do you hear me talking to you?" she asked through gritted teeth.

My eyes dropped to the floor as I struggled not to cry. I knew there was no way out—I looked guilty.

"Mom, you're right. I wasn't with Alexis, but that's only because she and Tameka left me and Angel to go off to some party. We were gonna spend the night at her place, but when they left us, we didn't feel like trying to go up to her house by ourselves," I offered weakly. Okay, so I'd managed to come up with a lie after all.

My mother's eyes narrowed. At first she didn't say any-thing. She just stood there with her hands on her hips, taking me in silently.

"We just thought it would be better if we went home instead of getting Alexis in trouble. Besides, her parents had been fighting so much, we decided not to stay there tonight. Ma, that's it," I said.

She blinked a few times. "Why are you sneaking in here like you've been out doing something you had no business doing?"

Dang, did mothers have crystal balls or something? Me and Walter had messed around some, nothing major because I definitely wasn't trying to have sex with him, but it was enough to have me feeling guilty.

"I didn't want to wake you up," I said, trying to come up with a good excuse. "I didn't know if you were sleeping or what was going on. Think about it, I could've just stayed at Alexis's and avoided all of this."

"One problem, Camille," she said triumphantly. "You never said a thing about spending the night out. If you were staying at Alexis's you would've taken a bag when you went out. You didn't. And since when did you decide when and where you were spending the night? Last time I checked, there was only one woman in this house, and her name ain't Camille."

I lowered my head and stared at the floor.

"Now if I find out you were out there with that boy I've warned you about, Camille, you mark my words, you will live to regret it!" she continued. "Now I'm only going to ask one more time, where were you tonight?"

I swallowed hard, finally deciding to try the truth, since she was always saying I'd get in less trouble if I was honest.

"Me and Walter were just hanging out."

My mother rubbed her forehead. "Hanging out? I thought I asked you to leave that boy alone. His mother has made it clear she does not want you involved with her son. And I don't want you in that situation."

"But, Mama, he's my boyfriend."

"Camille, did we or did we not go through this with Keith?"

I knew she was going to go there. She couldn't stand Keith. Just 'cause he'd been to jail, had a baby, cheated on me, and got me arrested.

"Mama, please understand."

"Camille, even if I did approve of this relationship, this boy is getting ready to go off to college clear across the country. His father is running in a very high-profile campaign. The last thing I want is people digging around in our business trying to find out about the little black girl he's dating."

"But—"

"But nothing! I don't want to hear any more about you dating this boy, do you understand? And as God is my witness, if you lie to me again, you won't leave this house until your eighteenth birthday!" She shot me a mean look before ordering me to my room.

16

Alexis

I knew everyone was going to have a million questions when I walked into the meeting tonight. I'd missed the last two meetings and hadn't been answering my cell phone. I hadn't even done my part for an upcoming talent show we were holding for the girls we mentored. Camille had even called me and left a message asking me to cover for her in case her mother called. I didn't get the message until today, and by then, my mom told me Mrs. Harris had already called. Oh, well. I hope Camille wasn't mad, but honestly, right now, I just couldn't worry about her.

I was totally depressed. Between my dad leaving and the fact that I hadn't even talked to Jaquan all week, I know I was messed up.

Surprisingly, it was my mom who had been trying to get me out of my funk. Of course, she wanted to go do something. But this time, it wasn't a trip to the spa or anything. We just went to the movies. I don't think either of us really paid any attention to the movie, though. But I guess it got us out of the house. Afterward, we went to Marble Slab for ice cream. We tried to talk about the divorce, but it wasn't doing anything but making us both sad all over again, so we changed the subject.

It was strange. I slept in my mom's bed last night. That was something I hadn't done since I was four years old. I'd heard her softly crying when I went to the kitchen to get something to drink in the middle of the night. I eased into the bed next to her. She put her arm around me and held me tight, and for the first time in a long time, I felt her love.

"Alexis!" Angel said, as I walked into the meeting room. "Girl, we were so worried about you."

"Yeah," Camille added. "We had already said we were coming over there after we left the meeting today."

"I'm okay," I said as I took a seat. "I've just been dealing with some things."

"What kind of things that you felt you couldn't talk to us about?" Camille said.

I sighed. I didn't have to worry about crying. I was all cried out.

"My parents are getting a divorce. My dad moved out," I said.

"I'm sorry to hear that," Camille said.

"Yeah," Jasmine added. "That's messed up."

"Tell me about it," I said. "What's going on?"

"We're just practicing for the auditions," Camille said. "You know we have the final audition this week."

Yeah, I knew. I just hadn't been motivated to do anything about it. Shoot, it looked like Tameka was going to get it anyway.

I thought about going to ask Dad to help me get the job, but then thought better of it. I didn't want anyone to accuse me of using my parent's wealth to get the position. Besides, with all the drama going on in our house, I kind of felt like my parents had better things to think about than me trying to get some TV job. Especially now.

When I mentioned the whole idea to my mother, a look of horror quickly spread across her face.

"What do you want a job for?" she asked.

"Mother, I'm not looking at it as a job. I just think it would be cool for me to do something like that, don't you?"

"That's the craziest thing I've ever heard. Why work when you don't have to?" she said.

My mother was a trip. The way she talked and carried herself these days, you'd think she was always born with the kind of money my father had. But the truth was, my mom's family was dirt-poor.

Sometimes I wish she would remember where she came from, because now she acts like she doesn't know what it is like to be without designer things.

"All I'm saying, dear, is if you need some money, your father and I would be happy to help. Besides, we don't want you to ruin your college chances by working. Then your grades will start to suffer. I think it best if you let one of those other girls get that job," she'd said.

I decided to focus on the job. Maybe that would help me forget what was going on at home.

We went through some practice rounds. Tameka got on everyone's nerves with her constant critiques, but all in all, we had a good session.

Afterward, I caught up with Jasmine as we walked out.

"Hey, Jasmine. Where's your brother?"

"Around, I guess," Jasmine said as she looked out in the parking lot, most likely looking for her ride.

"Oh, well, can you tell him to call me?" I wasn't sure, but I couldn't tell if she was being standoffish with me or what. I thought she was getting cool with the idea of me dating her brother.

"Look, I told y'all I don't want to be in the middle of nothing, a'wight?"

I looked at Jasmine funny. "Why you getting funky? I mean, I was just asking."

Before Jasmine could respond, her grandmother's car pulled up to the church. Her sister Nikki was driving this time. I smiled when I saw Jaquan in the passenger seat.

"Come on, Jasmine," Nikki yelled out the window. "I got to go. I'm gon' be late for work."

Jaquan got out of the car, smiling at me, looking all cute and stuff. "Hey, baby girl."

Jasmine rolled her eyes as she walked to the car.

"Boy, I ain't got time for you to be playing with your little girlfriend," Nikki snapped. "I got to go."

"Hey, Jaquan," I said, wishing Nikki would disappear.

Jaquan walked over and hugged me. "I'm sorry I've been so busy. We're getting ready for basketball season."

It felt so good to have him hug me.

Nikki blared the horn.

"Chill out!" Jaquan snapped.

"Why don't you tell her to go on?" I suggested. "We can go grab something to eat, then I can take you home." I knew it was eight-thirty and I probably should be getting back, but honestly, I wasn't looking forward to going home.

"You know, that sounds like the best thing I heard all day," he said. He turned to Nikki. "Beat it."

Nikki shook her head and started mumbling as she took off.

"You wanna drive?" I asked him, knowing how much he loved driving my car.

"You know it," he said, sticking out his hand.

I dropped the keys in his hand. "I need to be home by

ten, or my grandma will start trippin',” he said. “But let's go get something to eat. I just wanna spend a minute with my baby.” He leaned in and gently kissed me. We made our way to my car, and for the first time since my father left, I smiled.

17

Camille

We were all sitting in the makeup room at the station. The ladies had just added the finishing touches on me and started working on Jasmine.

"I like the colors they used on you," Alexis said to me.

"Hmm, I don't." Tameka snickered.

We all cut our eyes at her.

I looked at myself in the mirror. The two makeup artists were at the other end of the room. I doubt they could hear us because they had a CD playing in the background.

"What's wrong with my makeup?" I said, looking at myself in the mirror again.

"Well, everyone knows when you're dealing with TV you should put on more makeup than you'd normally wear."

"How does everyone know this?" Alexis asked.

"It's just common knowledge. That's why they have studio makeup. You know, that stuff that's really thick and gooey. It's like that for a reason, you know," Tameka said as she applied more lipstick to her already bright lips.

"Well, I think you look just fine," Alexis said to me.

"She would say that. But honestly, Alexis, your makeup needs a bit more work, too," Tameka said. She jumped up from her stool. I glanced down toward the makeup artist, who was still busy working on Jasmine.

"Here, let me show you guys what I mean." Tameka grabbed an old magazine from a table. She flipped through the pages until she arrived at one with models in it.

"Now, look at these models. You see their makeup? They're not wearing those dull colors. Those brown and earth colors. Look for yourselves if you don't believe me."

She pushed the magazine forward so that Alexis and I could get a better look.

"That's why I told them what colors to use on me. I wasn't about to let them mess up my chances by putting any ol' thing on my face," she bragged as she admired her reflection in the mirror.

I didn't know whether Alexis believed what she was saying, but she and I looked at each other, then down at the pictures of the models in the magazine.

"She looks like a druggie, with those dark circles around her eyes," I said.

"Yeah, look at this one." Alexis pointed to another thin model, whose makeup was similar to the first model's.

"That's not the point," Tameka snapped. "The point

is, they are completely made up. They're not just wearing a little makeup, because the camera can be hard on your skin. I mean, it shows all of your imperfections, so you need to overdo it almost. Plus, my cousin at CNN told me you have to do this because the light washes out your makeup, especially on women of color." She looked at us and shrugged. "But y'all do what you want."

When I looked at Tameka's face, I did notice she had applied even more foundation than what the makeup people had put on her. She took one more look at us, then walked off laughing and shaking her head.

When the makeup artist finished working on Jasmine, she came down to our end of the room.

"What's wrong with y'all?" she asked immediately.

"Nothing, girl, just tripping off something Tameka said," I replied.

"What now?" Jasmine asked as she surveyed her reflection in the mirror.

As Alexis filled Jasmine in on what Tameka had said, I picked up some of the brushes and started dabbing more makeup on my eyes. Soon the three of us were at the mirror, trying to add more layers on top of what the professionals had already done.

It wasn't until we heard Rachel's voice that we stopped and realized what we were doing.

"Girls, why are you still in here? Everyone has been waiting for you guys!" When we turned around, shock was all over her face. "Oh, my goodness! What happened in here?"

I shrugged and looked in the mirror. "What?"

"I thought the makeup artists fixed you guys up. What happened?"

Alexis looked at me, and I looked at Jasmine. "Is something wrong?" I asked.

"Well, I just mean, your makeup, it just looks like, um . . ."

"Like what?" Alexis asked.

"They put this on you guys?" Rachel just kept staring at us in amazement.

"We just added to what they did," I said.

"Why would you do such a thing?"

"Well, Tameka said we didn't have on enough makeup," Alexis answered. "She said we wouldn't look good on camera if we didn't add more makeup." She motioned toward the open magazine. "You know, like the models in the magazines."

"Girls, I don't think they wanted you looking like clowns," she said, pointing to our faces.

Shereen poked her head into the makeup room.

"C'mon, ladies, it's showtime," she said. When I turned around, the look on her face said it all.

"What in the world?" She opened the door and stepped into the room.

We all felt like fools.

She looked at her watch, let out a deep breath, and shook her head. "I don't even want to know. Let's go. You girls are late, and everyone's waiting."

She rushed out of the room and we followed, all of us trying desperately to wipe some of the makeup off with our hands. I looked at Jasmine. That was only making her look worse. I stopped, because I could only imagine what I was making mine look like.

When we walked into the room past Tameka and the producers, I was fuming. Tameka sat there looking like all innocent. She had wiped some of her makeup off and looked really natural. I wanted to wring her neck.

Me, Jasmine, and Alexis all threw her a nasty look as we walked by. We were supposed to tape a mock show with each of us taking turns as hosts, then guests.

The producers immediately shuffled us onstage. Bernadette, who was standing there with a clipboard, looked at us all crazy, I'm sure wondering what was wrong with our faces.

I shook my head. Tameka didn't know who she was messing with. She wanted to play dirty? Oh, I was about to show her dirty—and before it was all over, Tameka was going to wish she hadn't messed with me or my friends.

18

Alexis

I applied my last little touch of lip gloss and took another look in the mirror. Even I had to admit, I was looking too cute.

As I looked at my reflection, I thought back to yesterday's auditions. Things hadn't turned out that bad after all. Tameka had tried to make us look crazy, but we all managed to blow her off and have a pretty good audition. In fact, Camille had shocked everyone when she used her time as host to ask Tameka why she would stoop to cheating and trying to con people in order to get the job. It had left Tameka speechless. And Camille was so smooth with how she kept things flowing, going on to talk about how it doesn't matter whether you win or lose but how you play the game. I'd wanted to high-five her right there in the middle of the show.

I snapped out of my thoughts when I heard Jasmine groan. She was stretched out across the sofa in my room, impatiently waiting on me. We were going to a step show at Willowridge High School, which was about fifteen minutes away. But seeing as how we still had to go pick up Camille and the show started in ten minutes, we were definitely going to be late.

"I wish you'd hurry up," Jasmine groaned.

"Let me just pop some curls in the back of my hair, then I'll be ready," I said, as I turned on the curling iron.

"Look, I could've been at home writing on my research paper. I only have about three more pages to go. All the time I'm wasting here, I could've finished it," Jasmine said.

"Oh, be quiet. It's Friday night. Who wants to do homework on a Friday?" I responded.

"Just hurry up," Jasmine said as she stood up. "I'm going to use the restroom, and it would be great if you were ready to go when I get back."

"Take your time," I called out behind her.

She waved me off as she made her way into the bathroom.

I parted my hair and was just about to curl a section when my mother stuck her head into my room.

"May I come in?" she asked.

"Hey, Mom," I said.

"Where are you getting ready to go?" she said as she walked into the room.

"I told you earlier this week I was going to the Willowridge High School step show."

"Oh, yeah."

I was sure my mother didn't remember, but since I was in no mood to argue with her, I didn't say anything.

"So, who are you going with?" my mother asked as she plopped down on the sofa.

"Jasmine and the rest of the girls from the Good Girlz." I picked up the hot curling iron and brought it to my hair.

"Well, you have a good time, but I'm hoping you aren't going with that boy, Haquan."

I spun around toward her, hoping she didn't go there again.

"Mother, please. You know his name is Jaquan."

"No, you please. Don't tell me you're still talking to that thug Jaquan, Haquan, all those ghetto names are the same."

"Mama, you don't even know Jaquan." I lowered my voice and looked toward the bathroom door, praying that Jasmine couldn't hear us.

"I know enough to know that he is not the type of boy I want you spending your time with. He lives in public housing, for Christ's sake."

"And? What does that have to do with anything?"

"You know how those people are!"

"No, Mother. I don't know how those people are. And by the way, who exactly are 'those people'?"

My mother got this flustered and embarrassed look on her face before replying. "Look, you know what I mean.

I'm not trying to put anyone down, but you need to surround yourself with positive people."

"How do you know Jaquan isn't positive?" She was really pushing it now.

"Well, shall I say, people with similar goals and backgrounds. You go hanging out with that boy, and one of his dope-dealing friends will end up shooting you in the head trying to send a message."

I looked at my mother, waiting for her to start laughing or something. She couldn't possibly be serious. But the expression on her face told me that she was.

I shook my head and turned back to curling my hair.

"Lexi, I'm just looking out for your best interest," my mother continued. "Why would you surround yourself with people that can't do anything for you but bring you down? You see what happened to your friend Camille after hanging around with those low-class people. She got probation out of the deal. What are you going for, hard time?"

I could not believe my mother was sitting in my bedroom talking about me and my friends, and with Jasmine in the next room.

"Mother, could you please lower your voice," I whispered. "Jasmine's in the bathroom. She might hear you."

"Too late," Jasmine said walking out of the bathroom. Her eyes looked red, like she was fighting back tears.

I jumped up. "Jasmine, I'm so sorry. My moth—"

She held up her hand to cut me off. "Mrs. Lansing, I agree with you that Alexis shouldn't be dating my brother. I even tried to tell her that. However, and I ain't trying to be disrespectful but I'm one of *those* people. And would like to think that I am good enough to date anyone that steps to me, and so is my brother. Alexis is in no more danger being my friend than she is hanging around all those snobby girls at her private school, you know, the ones who got her caught up in their little boosting ring."

Jasmine's voice was cracking. I was a little shocked that she brought up the whole shoplifting fiasco that had landed us in trouble earlier this year. That was a little messed up, even for Jasmine. But I guess that meant she was really mad.

My mother really did look apologetic, but Jasmine didn't seem to care.

"We may not have the designer clothes, or the biggest bank account, but we ain't lacking for nothing," Jasmine continued as she started gathering her things. "Just because your family has more money doesn't make you any better than us." She threw her backpack over her shoulder. "Alexis, I don't feel like going out no more," she said. "I'll talk to you later."

"Where are you going?" I asked as she headed toward the door.

"Home. I saw a bus stop at the entrance to your subdivision. I'll just catch the bus." She headed down the stairs.

"At least let us take you home," my mother said, running after her. "It's getting late."

Jasmine spun around at the top of the staircase. "No, thank you, Mrs. Lansing. The buses run until nine. Besides, we wouldn't want you to have to take your Escalade into the 'hood."

With that Jasmine spun off, leaving me and my mother standing in the hallway with our mouths hanging open.

19

Camille

*W*hat are you trying to say, girl!" Jasmine snapped at Angel.

"I didn't say you were a hoochie. I said the leggings make you look like one!" Angel shrugged. I rubbed my head. Lately it seemed like all we did was fight. Alexis and Jasmine had spent the first twenty minutes arguing about something Alexis's mother did last night. I didn't get all of the details. I just know when Alexis arrived to pick me up for the step show, she was in a funk, and Jasmine was nowhere to be found.

They'd finally called a truce today after Alexis apologized for the trillionth time. Now we were sitting in the church meeting room, waiting on Rachel to finish youth choir rehearsal so we could start our meeting. Shereen was coming by to tape us in what she called a "natural environment."

"Well, I don't know who told y'all to dress like that, anyway. When I said stylish, I didn't mean look like you were auditioning to be on BET," Tameka said as she adjusted herself in her chair. She had on a cute long-sleeved top and some black slacks.

I looked down at my miniskirt and baby-doll top. Jasmine had on some black leggings and an off-the-shoulder midriff top. Alexis had on a skintight T-shirt.

"You said that Rachel told you to tell us to make sure we dressed like we were going to a party, because this was a socially themed show. And you said your cousin also said that," Alexis said.

"No." Tameka shook her head. "I said *don't* dress like you're going to a party."

"Tameka, I'm sick and tired of you and all your little sneaky ways," Jasmine screamed. "You were the one who told us that we looked more like we were going to church than to an audition for a teen show host. Then you started talking about all the tight outfits you saw on BET when you were watching videos."

Tameka jumped up, coming face-to-face with Jasmine. "Look, it ain't my fault y'all don't know nothing. I'm sitting here trying to help y'all out, and instead of being appreciative, you all trying to gang up on me. Didn't nobody tell you to wear those tired leggings, looking like you're in the Hoochie Mama of the Year contest," she snapped.

I was just as mad as Jasmine. I think I was more mad for even listening to Tameka again. She looked all professional, and we looked like we were going to the club. Nobody really wanted to listen to her, but after the way the producers and the intern had raved over her, I think all of us thought she halfway knew what she was talking about.

"I'm just sick and tired of your mess," Jasmine screamed at Tameka.

"Well, what you gon' do about it? You make me sick, Jasmine. You act like somebody owes you something. You all need to just realize that I'm the best person for this job and let it go," Tameka countered.

"If the best person is the one who can lie, cheat, and do whatever it takes to get the job, then I guess you are the best person for the job," Jasmine said.

Tameka and Jasmine were at a standoff, staring each other down.

"Like it's my fault y'all can't handle a little friendly competition," Tameka said, finally backing down.

"Competition is one thing, but flat-out lying and cheating to get what you want, that's just dirty," I tossed at her.

"Is that the only way you think you can win?" Jasmine snapped. "You're so scared that you can't win this fair and square that you have to stoop to scamming people."

"Whatever, Jasmine. It's not like you even stand a chance anyway," Tameka responded.

Before anybody could blink, Jasmine had pushed Tameka so hard, she fell to the ground. Me and Alexis jumped up at the same time to try and grab Jasmine before she pounced on Tameka.

Before we could get Jasmine calmed down, Tameka had stood up and rushed toward Jasmine. She grabbed Jasmine's hair, and both of them tumbled to the floor, this time Alexis going right with them.

Me and Angel had just reached down to try and break them up again when Rachel came storming into the room.

"What in the world is going on in here?" she screamed.

We quickly fell all over each other trying to get up from the floor.

"This makes no sense whatsoever!" Rachel said as she reached down to help me up. "I'm so tired of the bickering and arguing that's going on over this stupid teen show. It's all you guys talk about these days. And look at this foolishness. How much you wanna bet this fight has something to do with the show?" She huffed in frustration. "You all are up here acting like a bunch of hooligans, like you don't have any home training. And all over who's going to win this job."

Me, Alexis, Jasmine, and Angel all lowered our heads in shame.

"Auntie Rachel, I don't know why they don't like me." Tameka's whole tone had changed. She was whining like a little girl. And where had those tears come from? She was so full of it.

"I was just trying to help them out with some advice and Jasmine all but attacked me," Tameka quickly added.

"Save it, Tameka. I was born in the morning, but it wasn't this morning. I know you're not innocent in all of this."

It was Tameka's turn to look down at the floor. I was glad Rachel was finally letting her have it.

"And Jasmine, you know better than to put your hands on anybody! I've told you girls, violence doesn't solve a single thing. I'm so ashamed of all of you! Sit down!"

We all made our way back to our seats. I knew there was no point in trying to defend myself or the girls with Rachel being as mad as she was. So I took my seat and didn't say a word.

Rachel was right. We hadn't said or done a thing about our community service program. Lately all we'd been concerned about was the teen show. Even Angel, who wasn't even auditioning had gotten all wrapped up in trying to help someone win.

I knew things had gotten out of hand, but I definitely wasn't prepared for what came out of Rachel's mouth next.

"Y'all think I'm playing. If I hear about one more problem stemming from this teen show job, I'll personally tell Shereen that she should open it up to one of the nearby high schools, because it's obvious to me that you ladies can't handle this!"

"Miss Rachel," I protested. "You can't do that."

"Watch me. Any more problems, just watch me!"

Rachel was cool and all, but the look on her face said she meant business. One more problem, and all of us could forget about hosting anything.

20

Camille

$\mathcal{I}$ wasn't about to fall for any more of Tameka's stupid tricks. I think we had all figured out that while she was always trying to act like she was helping, all she was really doing was trying to make us look crazy.

As Jasmine and I walked into our English class, we were talking about the letter Tameka had started circulating around school. She was begging people to vote for her in this competition. There wasn't even a voting section of the auditions, but she was asking people to sign a "support petition."

"She must've accidentally slid this one into my locker," Jasmine said as she held out the flyer, complete with a color picture of Tameka all dressed up and holding a microphone.

"Dang, she's really going all out for this, huh?" I said.

"Yeah, the girl is serious. I mean, I want the job too, don't get me wrong, but we swore we wouldn't let this ruin our friendship, and here she goes trying every underhanded thing she can think of," Jasmine said. She pulled the door open and walked into the classroom. Tameka was sitting in the back and stared at us coldly when we walked in.

Jasmine walked over to her seat, which was right next to Tameka's. She rolled her eyes, then sat down.

"Okay, class. This is D day, as in due day. I need all of your research papers, and I need them now, minus the excuses of course!" our English teacher, Mrs. Lacy, snapped in her usual no-nonsense tone.

There was no noise except for the sound of backpacks being unzipped and people digging into their bags for their research papers.

I glanced over my shoulder to see Jasmine frantically flipping through her book bag. She slapped her forehead and started looking through the bag again. I looked over at Tameka, who had this grin across her face. I turned around and handed my research paper to the student Mrs. Lacy had picking them up.

"Miss Jones, is there a problem?" Mrs. Lacy must've noticed the frantic look on Jasmine's face.

Everyone turned to look at Jasmine.

"Um, I can't seem to find my paper," she sulked.

"Oh, is that so?" Mrs. Lacy said.

"No, seriously. I don't know what happened to it," Jasmine offered.

"Maybe the dog ate it," Tameka mumbled loud enough

for others to hear. The classroom broke into laughter. I turned to look at Jasmine, and I could see her eyes beginning to pool with water. I felt bad for her.

"I know she did it, because we worked on ours together," I said, trying to help.

Mrs. Lacy looked at me sternly. "I don't believe anyone asked for your input, Miss Harris."

"I promise you. I did my paper. I just can't find it right now," Jasmine pleaded. She emptied out her backpack. "And the jump drive I saved it on is gone, too!"

"Of course it is," Mrs. Lacy said as she walked toward the back of the room. She stood between Jasmine's row and the wall. "Well, it looks to me like you'll have to suffer the consequences since you can't 'find' this research paper you worked so hard on," she said. "Who else can't seem to find their research paper?" Mrs. Lacy asked as she looked around the room. She turned back to Jasmine. "Looks like you're the only one in class whose paper miraculously vanished into thin air," she said. She scooped up the remaining research papers, then walked up to the front of the classroom.

Jasmine looked like she wanted to cry, and I couldn't blame her. I knew how hard she had worked on that paper. We both did, because it was 30 percent of our grade. And with her getting an F on that last test, she had to do good on this paper. After class I waited outside for her. Mrs. Lacy had dismissed everyone except Jasmine.

"What did she say?" I asked, the minute Jasmine came out of the classroom.

"She said she wasn't buying my excuse for a second. She also told me that regardless of when I turn the paper in now, the most I can get is a C. This is messed up," Jasmine said sadly.

"Did you save it somewhere else?" I asked.

"No. You know I typed it in the library, and you can't save on the school's hard drive. I saved it on my jump drive, and I can't find that either."

I just nodded because I didn't know what else to say.

"She's giving me a week to turn in another one, so you know what that means, right?"

"Yeah, I guess you'll be swamped for the next week," I said.

"Um, try I won't be doing the show. Without at least a B on that research paper, my GPA goes down," Jasmine said with tears rolling down her cheeks. It was hard for me to watch her cry, because I could count on one hand the number of times I'd seen Jasmine cry.

All I could do was give her a hug. I didn't know what I could possibly say to help her feel better. And as badly as I wanted to win the hosting job, I felt really bad that she'd have to drop out.

I made up my mind then that I'd do whatever I could to help her redo her paper. It might be too late for the show, but the last thing we wanted was Jasmine failing a class.

21

Alexis

I couldn't believe how nervous I was. When Rachel called and said she wanted to call an emergency meeting with the Good Girlz, I was hoping she wasn't going to say she'd decided to stop the auditions. Better yet, wouldn't it be great if she told us that I had been selected as the host of the teen show? That would serve Tameka right for all the stupid stuff she'd been up to lately.

I was outside Madison, waiting to pick up Angel and Jasmine. I'd talked to Camille last night and she was just as nervous as I was.

My thoughts quickly faded when I saw Jaquan waving to me. He raced over and planted a big kiss on my lips.

"Hey, baby. I can't stay long. I gotta get to practice!" Jaquan said. "Jasmine told me you were picking them up. I'm glad I got a chance to see you." He kissed me again. "But I'll holla at you later."

Just that fast, he was gone. I smiled, taking note of the

fact that Jasmine had told him I'd be at their school. I took that to mean she was getting more and more comfortable with us dating.

I parked on the street outside their school and waited on Angel and Jasmine. I honked when I saw them walk out.

It had been a week since Jasmine's nightmare with the research paper. She had turned her new paper in earlier in the day, and we were all looking forward to going to the mall—that is, until Rachel called and told us she needed to see us right away.

"What do you guys think this is about?" Angel asked after they settled into the car.

Jasmine shrugged, like she didn't care. She was probably still mad that she had to drop out because of the research paper. I can understand that. Shoot, I'd be mad, too.

"I don't know, but I'm thinking it has to be pretty serious for her to call us in for a meeting, huh?" Angel said.

"Yeah, I guess so," I offered. "You know, I'll be glad when they announce a winner. I kinda agree with Miss Rachel—this thing has us trippin'. It's like that's all we think or talk about these days. I'll be glad when it's all over."

We all remained quiet as we made our way to the church.

"Where's Camille?" Jasmine finally asked. "I didn't see her after school."

"I think she said Walter was going to drop her off," Angel reported.

"Those two act like they're joined at the hip," Jasmine mumbled.

By the time we pulled up to the church, we saw Tameka strolling into the building. Even without her backstabbing, no matter how much I tried to click with her, something about her just didn't feel right to me. I couldn't put my finger on it, but it was something about her that made me not want to trust her.

The three of us walked in. We spoke to Camille, who was already there, then took seats in the back.

"Okay, now that everyone is here," Rachel began, "I wanted to remind you all that the girls we mentor will be here this weekend for the etiquette workshop. I hope each of you is ready for your part."

We all looked at Rachel like she was crazy. I know she didn't call an emergency meeting for that. We'd talked about that at our last meeting, and we were all prepared.

Rachel smiled, like she knew she was torturing us. "Okay, that's not the only reason we're here. I'll get to the real reason for this meeting in a minute. But first, let me start by saying, I want you all to know I believe all of you are quite capable of doing this job. Unfortunately, they only need one person, and that has made things very difficult around here. I'd like us to take a moment and pray that whatever happens, we'll continue to work together to complete God's mission. Remember, this show is not about us. It's about what we're here to do for others. Now before we do anything, let's say a prayer."

Rachel bowed her head and started praying. I don't think any of us could really concentrate because we wanted to know what this was all about.

Thankfully, she made it quick, then turned her attention back to us. "Shereen wanted to be here, but she had an important meeting, so she had me make the announcement," Rachel continued. "Well, the moment you all have been waiting for. The network executives have made a decision, sort of."

I held my breath. I just wanted her to spit it out.

"They've narrowed down the candidates to two girls. They're going to make a final decision in a couple of weeks after they see a little more from the finalists." She smiled.

"Again, this is not a reflection on any of you, it's just that they can only pick one person," Rachel said.

"Miss Rachel, please, can you please just tell us!" Camille blurted out. I was just glad she said what I was thinking.

"Oh, yeah, well, the producers have chosen Alexis and Camille as the two finalists for the host of *Teen Talks*," Rachel said.

"What!" Tameka screamed.

"What!" Camille repeated.

"Oh, my God," I said.

Everyone started talking at once.

"I can't believe this!" Tameka jumped from her chair. "Somebody cheated!" she screamed.

Every head turned toward her.

"That somebody would be you." Jasmine laughed. "But I guess it didn't work."

"This is some bull!" Tameka snapped.

"Tameka, you should calm down," Rachel said.

Tameka ignored her. "I can't believe they picked these two." She pointed at me and Camille. "Over me!" She was obviously disgusted. "This was rigged from the very start. I should've known they were gonna favor someone who'd been with this stupid group from the very beginning."

"Tameka, this was nothing personal. You knew when you entered the competition that only one person would win," Rachel tried to reason. "We had nothing to do with the finalists they chose. Now you need to take your seat and try to be happy for Camille and Alexis."

"Be happy? Why? When I was robbed. This is crazy," she ranted.

"I can't believe you're acting like this," Rachel said. "Why can't you be happy for the other girls?"

"They probably picked her 'cause her daddy got some money," Tameka said, pointing at me. She then shook her head and threw up her hands.

"Tameka, I will tell you again. Sit down and settle

down," Rachel said, a lot more calmly than I would have. "Everyone was interested in the position. Don't take this so personally."

"You don't understand how hard I've worked for this," Tameka cried.

"All of you worked hard. Everyone worked hard and did their best. That's what I wanted to tell you. Although you were not selected, you did a great job. Everyone did," Rachel said.

"I think we should just focus on helping Alexis and Camille," Jasmine tossed in, a smile across her face. You could tell she was happy about the outcome.

Tameka looked at her. "Oh, you just shut up! You're just jealous because losing your stupid research paper on DuBois got you disqualified."

Jasmine's smile quickly faded. "How did you know what my research topic was?" Jasmine scooted to the edge of her seat.

The room grew silent as everyone waited for Tameka to answer.

"Because you said it," Tameka stammered.

Jasmine stood up. "No. I didn't."

"You must have. How else would I have known?" Tameka tried to plaster an innocent look on her face.

Jasmine turned to me. I gave her a look to let her know that I hadn't said anything.

"Jasmine, please sit down," Rachel said with a huge sigh.

Jasmine sat down, but with the glare she was shooting Tameka, I knew this was far from over. If Tameka had taken that research paper, I felt sorry for her. Because payback from Jasmine definitely wasn't going to be pretty.

22

Camille

$\mathcal{W}$alter was such a gentleman. That's what I was thinking as I sat patiently in the passenger side of his car and waited for him to come and open my door. We had just pulled up to Dave and Buster's to hang out and play some games.

When he opened the door, I tried my best to step out of the car graciously. All I could think about was how perfect we would be if only our parents would stop trippin'.

Inside, we played a few games before sitting down to order some appetizers. "Hey, congrats on being selected for the show," Walter said after we'd placed our orders.

"I haven't won yet. It's between me and Alexis."

"Yeah, I know, but I think you would be great at it. I mean, think about it." He shrugged. "I think it would be cool to have my girlfriend as a big TV star." He chuckled.

Walter's dimples were really deep, especially when he laughed. I loved how he kept referring to me as his girl, or his girlfriend. I thought about it and realized we never really discussed going together. It was like one day we just started kickin' it and we've been together ever since. We were together as much as possible. I still spent time with the girls, but most of my time was spent with Walter.

The snap of Walter's fingers brought me back to our conversation.

"Hey, you daydreaming on me or something? Our waiter asked if you wanted anything else," Walter said.

I shook my head. "Sorry, I was just lost in thought." I looked up at the waiter, who seemed like he had an attitude.

"I'm okay. I don't want anything else. Thank you," I said.

"You sure?" Walter asked.

"Yeah, I'm good."

He looked at the waiter. "Okay, then I guess I'll just take the check."

When the waiter left our table, Walter leaned in closer to me. "You know, my dad sits on the community advisory board over at Channel 2."

I looked at him, wondering just where he was going with this conversation.

"And?"

"And, well, I was just thinking, if you really wanted the job, I could make sure you get it." He shrugged and eased back to his side of the table.

"Your parents don't like me, though."

"It's just my mom trippin'. My dad could care less. He just wants to do anything to make me happy. And seeing you as the host would make me very happy."

The idea swirled around in my mind. Was what he was saying really possible? Could he simply ask his dad to help me out, and I'd get the job? Would that even be right? I smiled at the thought of me being on TV, hosting my very own talk show. Then there's the money issue. Five whole hundred Benjamins a week? Man, how much would that be a month, or a year even? I could get my own apartment, or maybe even a newer car, and get rid of that beat-up old Toyota Corolla that my mom never lets me drive anyway.

"You keep blanking out on me, girl," Walter said.

"Oh, I'm sorry. It's just that I was thinking about the job. I really, really want it," I said.

"Well, I can really, really talk to my dad for you," he said, playfully mocking me. "I mean, I'm sure I could convince him to put in a good word for you."

Again, I thought about it. I mean, what if Alexis had her dad pull a few strings for her? Wouldn't this be like the same thing? Everyone knows how rich her parents are. Who would care if Walter's dad said a few good things about me? And who's to say his dad would even help?

As we walked to the car hand in hand, Walter asked if I wanted to go over to the Galleria Mall, which was about ten minutes away. He said he wanted to check out the new tennis shoes by LeBron James.

We made our way into the mall and then to the shoe store. When I saw Walter salivating over those shoes, I realized that I wanted to buy them for his birthday, which was next month. The problem was, I had twenty bucks to my name. That got me to thinking again just how much this job could help. So now I was feeling like I not only wanted the job, I needed it.

Walter looked at me and asked, "What do you think?"

"Yes."

He looked at me crazy.

"Yes?" he questioned.

"Yes, I want your help," I said.

"My help? I was asking what you think about the shoes." He glanced down at his feet.

For the first time I realized he had the tennis shoes on. I laughed at myself for being so caught up in thoughts about that job that I didn't even realize what he was talking about.

"Oh, yeah, those look good, too. But I was talking about the job," I confessed.

"So you want my help?"

I nodded.

He smiled, showing off those dimples again.

"Okay, I'll talk to my dad as soon as I get home, but what about the LeBrons?" he asked, turning his foot from left to right so I could get a better look at the shoes.

"They're all right, but I don't know that they're worth a hundred and thirty dollars," I said.

"You're probably right," he said as he sat down and began taking them off.

I didn't want Walter to get the shoes because I wanted to get them for him. I *would* get them for him. Now all I had to do was get the job so I had a way to pay for them.

23

Alexis

I was sitting in Jasmine's living room, trying to pretend I didn't hear her mother lecturing her in the kitchen about the importance of keeping her grades up. After she finally turned in her research paper on W. E. B. DuBois, she got a C-minus, and her mother wasn't too thrilled.

"You've gotta keep in mind that you are setting an example for the others to follow. What are your brothers supposed to think if you can't keep your grades up?" Her mother sighed. "I agreed to let you take part in that group only if you kept up your grades, but now with your teachers calling about you missing assignments and things like that, I'm wondering if that's even a good idea," she continued.

"Ma, I am keeping my grades up. I don't understand why Mrs. Lacy even called you. I told her I did the stupid paper, I just couldn't find it." Jasmine leaned back in her chair and pouted. "Then when I finally did the paper and turned it in, she gives me a C-minus. It was like she was still punishing me for not having it the first time around. I don't think that's fair."

Jasmine's grandmother was yelling at one of her brothers down the hall. Her mother sipped from her coffee mug and looked at her. "Why didn't you just turn the paper in on time in the first place? You and that friend of yours worked hard on those research papers. I was so disappointed when I found out you went to class without it."

"I don't know what happened. It was in my book bag in my room, and when I got to class and tried to find it, I couldn't. See, this is why we need a computer here. If I had my own computer, I would've just been able to print it out again."

"Jasmine, I've told you, we can't afford a new computer right now. Your grandmother and I have been talking about getting one, but it won't be until close to Christmas. You need to be thankful for the things you do have and not worry about what you ain't got, you hear me?" Her mother shot her a chastising look.

"Yeah, Ma," Jasmine said.

"Excuse you?"

"I mean yes, ma'am."

Her mother got up to refill her coffee cup. "Where's Jaquan? He know he got this girl waiting." She motioned toward me.

"You the one made him go to the store, Mama," Jasmine said.

I laughed. I loved Jasmine's family. They were so funny, and as much as she complained about them, it seemed like they had a lot of love.

"Oh, did that girl ever get those papers she was looking for?" Jasmine's mother asked as she sat back down.

"What girl, Ma?" Jasmine asked.

"About two weeks ago, your little friend from the group came over. You had just left with Alexis, but she said you left some stuff in your room. Well, I didn't know what she was talking about, so I let her go in there and she came out with a folder, saying she found what she needed." Her mother leaned back and rubbed her feet. "It's so good to have a day off."

"Who came to my room to get a folder?" Jasmine asked, obviously trying not to hear about her mother's day off.

"I told you, it was one of those girls from the group. She said you were supposed to bring the papers for her, and you had forgotten them. So I let her go back and get them."

"Was it Angel or Camille?" Jasmine looked concerned.

"Oh, chile, no. I know who they are. This girl is new. I never saw her before. She told me all about the talk show competition and said you were supposed to bring the scripts to rehearsals. I figured it was okay. I took her back to your room, but then your brother slipped and fell in the bathroom, so I had to go see about him. By the time I got back she had found the folder and was rushing out of here."

"Ma, why didn't you tell me this before?" Jasmine looked like she was about to lose it.

"I just told you, your brother slipped and fell. That's the night we had to take him to the emergency room. There were other things on my mind than you guys forgetting your scripts," her mother said.

Jasmine took a deep breath, like she was trying to calm herself down. "Was her name Tameka?"

Her mother snapped her fingers. "Yes, she said she was new to the group." Her mom stood and headed out of the kitchen. "She said you guys were on your way to rehearsal when you called to say you had forgotten the scripts at home and asked her to pick them up. Now, I'm through being your personal secretary, and I'm going to lay down. Keep your brothers entertained and out of my hair for a while, please."

Jasmine didn't pay her mother any attention as she jumped up from the table and grabbed the phone.

"I cannot believe her!" She turned to me. "What's Tameka's number?"

I know Tameka was low-down, but I didn't think she'd go this far. "I don't know. You don't believe she actually stole your paper?"

"Yes, I do. I think she snuck into my room and stole my research paper. She saw my folder when I showed it to Camille at the meeting," Jasmine said. I stood next to her with my mouth hanging open. No way would Tameka be that bold.

"Think about it. This is Tameka we're talking about," Jasmine reminded me.

"That's how she knew what your paper was about when Miss Rachel announced the finalists for the show host. I can't believe her. What are you gonna do?" I said.

"Oh, trust, I am going to make her sorry she ever decided to mess with me, and that's a promise," Jasmine vowed as she slammed the phone back on the hook.

24

Camille

I was outside the church, talking to Walter. I had been about to go into tonight's meeting, but Walter had caught me on my cell phone as I was walking in. I had planned just to talk to him a minute, and even though I know he didn't mean to, he was making me a nervous wreck.

"Are you ready?" he asked.

"For?"

"Don't play silly with me. You're about to be named the new host of *Teen Talks*, aren't you excited?"

"Walter, we don't know that for sure. Alexis could still get it," I tried to reason. We'd had our final interviews yesterday. Alexis and I went separately and did an interview with Shereen and some other bigwigs. They also had us do some on-camera work on the spot. I don't know how Alexis did, because she went several hours before me. I'd tried to call her last night, but she wasn't answering her cell phone.

"We just have to wait and see who they pick," I added, bringing my attention back to my conversation with Walter.

"Well, my dad told me who got the job. If you don't want it, I could tell him to tell the board that you're not really interested," he teased. "Then I guess they could just go to the second runner-up, or maybe they could ask around," he said.

"Walter? Quit joking with me." I pouted. "I'm nervous enough as it is."

"Well, I just wanted to be the first to tell you how proud I am of you," he said.

A part of me didn't feel worthy of his praise, though. I know this may be strange, but as badly as I wanted the position, I felt a little weird knowing I only got it with his help.

"Okay, I'm here, let me call you back later," I said as I entered the room. Just about everyone was there. I guess they were just as anxious as me.

I was the last person to make it into the room. I tried to calm my nerves. As much as I wanted to win, I was really feeling bad about asking Walter to help. Now, if I did get the job, I'd never know if I could've won fair and square. Besides, Alexis was my girl. How had I gotten so caught up in winning that I'd do this to her?

"Okay, attention, everyone!" Rachel raised her voice, trying to get us to start our meeting. I took my seat, trying to shake off the sinking feeling in my stomach.

"As you know, the producers have made their decision about who will be the new host of *Teen Talks*. Now, again, I want to reiterate that all of you did a great job. Camille and Alexis, I understand your final interviews went well. I must say that I'm glad that we decided to stick with the process and see it all the way through." Rachel stopped talking and made eye contact with me. But the look on her face had me a bit scared. I just wanted this done and over with. I couldn't even look Alexis in the face.

Rachel flashed a big smile, then peeked into an envelope she held in her hands. She silently read the paper, but her expression didn't reveal a thing. I was hoping she'd look up at either me or Alexis as a clue, but she didn't. I thought about all the reasons why Alexis would get the job over me. Her parents were rich, and very well known. Shoot, her daddy could probably buy the TV station if he wanted. Maybe she had had him pull some strings. Nah—I shook my head. Alexis wasn't like that, which made me feel even more guilty.

"Without further delay," Rachel announced, "girls, please give your new *Teen Talks* host a round of applause. Introducing Camille Harris!"

When Rachel said my name, I just sat there and closed my eyes. I was so excited and happy, I didn't know what to do. Even though Walter had already told me that I had the job, it didn't set in until I heard it from Rachel's mouth.

Then, when everyone rushed me to offer up hugs, saying congrats, I knew that no matter what happened, from that moment forward my life would never be the same. I looked at Alexis. She looked genuinely happy.

"Girl, I knew you would get it. You're so much more talented than me. Congratulations." She reached in to hug me.

"Thank you," I whispered as I hugged her back.

As the other girls surrounded me, I couldn't help but say a small prayer for God to forgive me for the underhanded way I'd gotten the job.

25

Camille

$\mathcal{W}$e can call this the big celebration dinner," Walter said
to me as we pulled up in front of the Cheesecake Factory
in Sugar Land. I used the visor mirror to check my hair as
he walked around to open my door.

Exactly one week had passed since I was named host
for *Teen Talks*, and already I'd been interviewed by the
Houston Chronicle, the *Houston Press*, and *Seventeen* magazine. It was like I was a celebrity, and the show hadn't even
started yet.

Shereen told me that everything would move fast, and
next week the station was sending me on a shopping spree
to make sure I had all the right outfits for the program.
And I was going to have my hair done by the hairstylist
who does all the anchorwomen's hair here in Houston. It
was like I was living a fairy tale come true.

Then, to top it off, Walter was treating me like royalty.
When we walked up to the hostess in the restaurant, he

looked at her and said, "Yes, I made reservations for myself and the new host of Houston's hottest teen show, *Teen Talks*." And he was serious. I socked him in the arm.

"Quit playing," I said.

"Who's playing? I'm serious as a heart attack. You gotta let people know who you are."

The hostess giggled and pulled out two menus. "Follow me this way," she said.

As we walked to our table, she looked over her shoulder at me. "Are you really the new host for that show? We all heard about it. When is it starting up?"

"I am, and I think we're going to start shooting next week," I replied, trying to contain my excitement.

"Wow!" she said as she led us to a secluded table off in a corner of the restaurant.

"Is this okay?" she asked Walter.

He nodded and smiled. Then he reached for my chair and pulled it out.

"Well, congratulations on the job. Your waitress will be with you in a few moments," she said as we sat down. She placed our menus in front of us, smiled, then walked back up to the front of the restaurant.

"So how does it feel to be a star?" Walter asked.

"Please. It hasn't really started yet, but it was cool being interviewed by the paper and the magazine. They had this photographer come and snap a bunch of pictures of me. That was cool," I confessed.

Walter took my hands across the table. "You are really special, Camille, with or without your fancy new job."

He kissed my fingers, and I swear I felt on top of the world.

We ordered quickly and started talking about what I should expect as host of the show. When our food came, I was glad, but as I looked at the chicken and shrimp pasta, I made a note that I would have to start watching what I ate. I had just taken a bite when I looked up and almost choked.

"Are you okay?" Walter asked, his voice laced with concern. "Is it too spicy for you?" He quickly offered me my glass of water while I slapped my chest a couple of times.

"I do not believe this," I mumbled, trying to clear my throat. My eyes were watering when I looked up to make sure I was seeing what I thought I was seeing. I was. My ex-boyfriend, Keith, was walking toward our table. I wanted to disappear into thin air because I knew wherever Keith was, trouble was definitely close behind.

"What's wrong?" Walter asked again. This time he turned to see where I was looking.

"Walter, that's my ex. He's nothing but trouble. Just please, don't say anything to him," I begged.

"Dang, Camille. Why are you acting all scared? You don't have to worry about him while you're with me. You already know, I'm no scaredy suburban boy. We're together now. I'm sure he'll get the message soon enough," Walter said with confidence.

"You don't know Keith. Trust me, if he's here, it's because he's here to start up some trouble." I played with my food, suddenly losing my appetite.

Walter shook his head. "Don't worry about it," he said, and dug into his nachos.

Keith stopped right in front of our table. He didn't even look at Walter.

"Well, if it isn't my baby girl. I called you. Several times," Keith said as a huge smile crossed his face.

I wanted to ignore him. But I knew Keith. He wasn't one to be ignored. He looked as good as I last remembered. His smooth fade actually looked better than the Afro he'd worn for years. He definitely looked better than he did when we were together. I shook off my thoughts. "Hi, Keith. How's your baby mama?"

He chuckled. "LaShay is history, which is what I've been trying to tell you. If you'd have returned my calls, I coulda told you all about it."

"Ummph, too bad. Well, as you can see, I'm in the middle of dinner." I motioned to the table. "So see ya."

Keith glanced over at Walter. "So is this why you can't return my calls? Because you got jungle fever?"

I shook my head. "Not now, Keith," I tried to say calmly.

"Not now!" Keith hated to feel like somebody was blowing him off. "So when? I mean, I'm trying to be patient and all, but—" He took a deep breath. "Look, why don't you step outside so I can holla at you."

Walter stood up. He was about the same height as Keith, but Keith was a lot more muscular. "Look, dude, she doesn't want to be bothered," he said calmly.

Keith turned to Walter and threw him a crazy look.

"No, you look, *dude*. This is between me and my girl. Ain't nobody talking to you. Ya feel me?"

"Keith, I'm not your girl. I haven't been your girl in almost a year. Why are you trippin'?" I asked as I stood up.

Keith reached out and grabbed for my arm. "I told you, I just wanna holla at you for a minute."

I jerked my arm away, and two seconds later Walter pushed Keith. "I said, leave her alone!"

I didn't see where Keith's cousin Peanut came from, but all of a sudden he was at Keith's side.

"Yo, dawg, I know this fool didn't just push you." Peanut said. "You gon' let him punk you like that?"

By now, other customers were looking at us. I closed my eyes and prayed something would happen to make these two go away.

Keith brushed the front of his shirt and forced a smile. "I'ma let you make that one, Billy Bob. But if you ever put your hands on me again, your mama will be making funeral arrangements. Ya feel me?"

He didn't give Walter time to respond before he turned back to me. "So, Camille, you think you too good for a brother now?" He rubbed his chin. I could tell he was trying to calm himself down. "I saw the story the paper did on you. You 'bout to blow up, huh? And I guess that means you too good to call somebody back?"

"Keith, I really don't want to talk to you. We are over and done with," I said as I sat back down. "Walter, please sit down. Let's just finish dinner, and maybe Keith and his flunky cousin will go away."

Suddenly Keith grabbed me by my shirt and pulled me up from the chair. Before I knew what was happening, Walter jerked his arm, reached back, and slammed his fist dead into Keith's jaw.

People started screaming as Keith hit the floor. Two security guards immediately rushed to our table.

"What's going on here?" one guard asked as Keith struggled to get up.

"My boyfriend and I were trying to have dinner when these two showed up to start trouble," I quickly reported. The guards looked at Keith and Peanut. Keith looked like he was ready to charge Walter, but the guard's look must've made him think twice.

Walter, who had turned red from anger, leaned over and whispered something in one of the guard's ears.

"You two are gonna have to leave now," the guard said firmly after he listened to whatever Walter had to say.

Keith didn't flinch.

"Either that, or you go to jail," the guard warned.

Keith shoved the guard who had helped him up off of him and acted as if he were brushing dirt from his clothes.

"This ain't over, Camille," he snarled. "And you, *dude* . . ." Keith laughed. "Get your black suit ready." The guard escorted Keith and Peanut out.

I was wondering why we didn't get thrown out, too. I figured it was because of whatever Walter whispered to the guard. After the commotion died down, I kept apologizing to Walter. I felt so bad.

"Look, don't worry about it," he said as he rubbed his fist.

"But I'm so embarrassed."

"You don't have anything to be embarrassed about," Walter assured me.

"I don't like him threatening you."

Keith just tried to act tough. He wasn't really a thug, and I hoped that fear of going back to jail would keep him from doing anything stupid.

"I ain't worried about him." Walter tried to smile. "Let's just finish our food."

I wanted to forget about this whole fiasco, so I just let it drop. The rest of our evening went on without any more interruptions.

After dessert, Walter paid the check, and we started walking out to the parking garage. It was a nice evening, and I wasn't in any hurry to get back home. As we walked, holding hands, I stopped Walter and turned to face him.

"Again, I'm so sorry about what happened back there earlier. I want you to know that ever since we've been talking, I haven't said a word to Keith. It was long over between us before you even came into the picture," I said.

Walter took me into his arms and kissed me. We hugged for a while, then he said, "I know, Camille. And I can't blame him for wanting you back. But you're mine now."

We started toward the car. "Do you remember where we parked this time?" I asked, making fun of him because on our last date he couldn't remember where the car was. I was glad we were trying to put the disaster of our date behind us.

"Yes, c'mon, smart aleck. We're on the second level." I followed him to the right level, and we walked toward the car.

As Walter dug into his pocket for the keys, I couldn't help but look at him and smile. He unlocked the doors and opened mine for me to get in. I gave him a quick kiss and got in. Before Walter could get my door closed, I saw Keith come out of nowhere and tackle Walter to the ground. Then Peanut also came out of nowhere and started kicking Walter. Before I could get out of the car, they were kicking and beating Walter while he was on the ground. I didn't know what to do. I started screaming, then I jumped on Keith's back, but he pushed me to the ground and kept pounding away at Walter's head and face.

"Take that, punk!" he yelled as he landed a right hook to Walter's jaw. "Stay outta business that ain't yours!"

"Who's bad now?" Peanut laughed as he hit Walter in the side with a crowbar.

"Please, please, somebody, please call the police!" I screamed.

An elderly couple walking by finally tried to intervene, but by then it was too late. Keith and Peanut took off, and Walter lay on the ground, covered in blood. He was moaning. I took his head into my lap and held him until the police and an ambulance arrived.

26

Camille

I had been waiting in the emergency waiting room for over four hours now. Angel, Alexis, and Jasmine were there with me. I was a nervous wreck because I'd overheard the doctor telling Mrs. and Mr. Lewis that Walter had suffered a concussion, and things weren't looking good right now. If something happened to him, especially because of me, I would just die.

"Camille, c'mon. Please have a seat. Walter is going to be fine," Alexis said. I know she was just trying to help me stay calm, but she was getting on my nerves with that positive attitude. She didn't know if he was going to be all right or not.

I was about to tell her that when Walter's teary-eyed mother walked into the waiting room. Her husband was holding her up on one side, because she was walking like her body was limp. Walter's sister was holding her up on the other side. Mrs. Lewis looked over and saw me and must've found the energy to stand up, because she pulled herself away from her family and walked over to where I was standing.

"This is all your fault! My son is in there fighting for his life because of you!" she screamed at me. I could only stand there in shock as Alexis scooted up next to me and took my hand.

"Darling, please calm down," Mr. Lewis said, trying to ease his wife into a chair. She plopped down, buried her head in her hands, and began sobbing.

Mr. Lewis turned back to me. "Camille, as you can imagine, my wife is very upset."

"Is Walter going to be all right?" I could barely get the words out.

"We don't know," Mr. Lewis responded. "He was beaten pretty badly." He took a deep breath. "We need you to tell us what happened. The police would only say you two were leaving dinner when two men attacked him. Apparently these were the same two men you exchanged words with at the restaurant?"

I lowered my head. "It was my ex-boyfriend and his cousin."

Mrs. Lewis looked up and glared at me, her chest heaving up and down. "I told him! I told you were nothing but trouble." She began crying again as Walter's sister took her mother in her arms and tried to calm her down.

"How, I mean, what happened?" Mr. Lewis said. He, too, looked worn out; his eyes were beet red.

"I don't know. Keith just showed up at the restaurant, and him and Walter got into it, and security put Keith and his cousin out. We thought everything was fine until we were leaving," I cried.

Mrs. Lewis pulled herself away from her daughter, stood, and walked over to me. "I hope you're happy. First, you have my son lying to me—something he has never done until he met you. Then you use him to get you that job with the TV station, having my husband calling in favors to pull strings and get you the job. Now this!"

I stood there speechless, and when I felt Alexis release my hand, I knew my day had gone from bad to worse.

"What is she talking about?" Alexis whispered.

It was my turn to bury my face. "Not now, Alexis, please."

His mother must've realized what she'd done, because she formed a small smile. "Oh, she didn't tell you? She had my husband use his influence to get her the *Teen Talks* job. She wanted it so bad, she had my son beg his father to do something as unethical as that."

Alexis, Jasmine, and Angel stared at me with their mouths open.

Luckily, we were interrupted by the nurse, who stuck her head in the waiting room. "Mr. and Mrs. Lewis, your son is awake. Please come with me."

They both turned and took off out of the waiting room without another word to me. Walter's sister quickly followed behind them.

As soon as they left, Alexis, Angel, and Jasmine surrounded me.

"You had his father get you the job?" Alexis said, a look of disbelief across her face.

"That's messed up," Jasmine said before I could respond.

"Please tell us it's not true," Angel added.

I contemplated lying to them, but I was just too worn out to think up a lie. "It's not like that at all. I just, I mean, when Walter asked if I wanted his help, I said okay. It's not like I set him up to do it."

Alexis looked really hurt. "You know, I could've easily had my father make a donation or something, but I wanted this to be fair and square. And when you won, I was really happy for you."

"And to think, we thought Tameka would go to any lengths to get the job. You are foul, Camille," Jasmine added.

"Y'all it's not like that," I tried to plead.

"Whatever," Jasmine said, turning to Alexis and Angel. "Y'all ready to go?"

I didn't want them to leave because I didn't want to be at the hospital alone. But judging from the looks on their faces, there was nothing I could say right now to convince them to stay. That's why I didn't say a word as they shot me evil looks on their way out the door.

27

Alexis

So lemme get this straight, Jaquan. You're trying to tell me that you and your ex got back together, just like that?" I couldn't believe my ears. He was trying to dump me like I'm some little chicken head.

"Um, look, you're real cool, Alexis. But me and Tranita, we go way back. We went together in the eighth grade. I mean, we got history," he said.

I moved the phone from my ear and looked at it. He had to be kidding me. There are so many guys who'd love to be with me, and here he was telling me about history he and his ex-girlfriend had? I couldn't believe it. What I couldn't believe most, though, was how I had allowed myself to fall for him. And now he was sitting up here trying to weasel his way out of our relationship. I had called him to vent about Camille. I never expected to get this.

"Look, Alexis, I ain't got all night to be trying to explain this to you. Tranita is ready to go, I'll see you around," he said.

Imagine being dumped over the phone while your boyfriend's ex is standing by waiting on him to do it. Boy, was I mad. But I was more mad at myself. The truth was, I had really started feeling Jaquan. Not just because he was so cute, but because I really liked him. I knew Jasmine hadn't wanted us together in the first place, but things were finally working out. I thought she was getting used to the idea, and everything seemed like it was on the right track.

I sat around, trying to figure out what I was going to do. I didn't know if I should try to get him back or just move on. I knew Jaquan cared about me just as much as I cared about him. Tranita must've said something to worm her way back in. No, I decided. I wasn't letting go of Jaquan without a fight. I turned my ringer off, put on the CD with love songs he had made for me, and cried myself to sleep.

First thing the next morning, I rushed over to Jasmine's apartment. I already had it planned out. I was going to tell Jasmine I had stopped by so we could talk about what we were gonna do about Tameka and Camille. At first I wasn't too keen on payback, but now, working with Jasmine would give me a chance to find out what her brother was up to and implement my plan to get him back.

When I knocked on the door, Jasmine answered. But instead of inviting me in, she stepped out in the hall and pulled the door shut behind her. I found that strange, but I didn't say anything right off.

"Hey, what's up?" she asked.

"I was in the area and thought I'd stop by so we could talk about Tameka and Camille. You decided what to do to get her back yet?"

Jasmine shook her head. "Nah, I'm thinking of just letting that drop. Shoot, Tameka not getting the job is payback enough. And I don't even feel like dealing with Camille."

We stood there in the hall staring at each other. So much for my plan.

"What's wrong?" she finally asked.

"You just gon' let them off like that? Especially Tameka?"

She shrugged. "I don't know. I'm just not really trippin' off Tameka right now."

"Oh. Well, what's going on with you?" I wondered if she knew me and Jaquan had broken up.

"Jaquan told me, Alexis," Jasmine blurted out, answering my question.

I swallowed hard, then looked at her.

"What did he tell you?" I asked, still trying to figure out why we were standing out in the hallway. I can't remember a time when Jasmine wouldn't let me into their apartment. Even if it wasn't clean, she'd be like, "Oh, excuse the mess."

Jasmine sighed. "He told me y'all broke up. And well, I don't think it's a good idea for you to come in. Tranita is here, and I really don't want any mess," she said.

My heart sank. "Why is she here this early?" It was only ten o'clock.

Jasmine cocked her head. "Why are *you* here this early?"

"Did she spend the night?" I couldn't believe how worked up I was getting.

"Now you know my granny ain't even having that."

"Let me ask you a question. When did they get back together?"

Jasmine lowered her head and didn't say anything.

"Was he messing with her while we were together?" I cried.

Jasmine wouldn't answer, but the look on her face said it all.

"He was cheating on me, and you knew it! Why didn't you say anything to me?"

Jasmine threw her hands up. "This is why I didn't want y'all messing around in the first place, because I didn't want to get caught up in any of this drama."

"You still should have told me. You are supposed to be my friend."

"Look, Alexis. Even though I can't stand my brother, I still can't sell him out by telling all his business."

I knew Jasmine could see the water pooling in my eyes.

Not only did her words hurt, it also hurt that she didn't want to let me in. I wanted to see Jaquan's girlfriend. I wanted to know if she looked better than me. I wanted to know what it was about her that made him go back to her without even giving us a good chance.

"I'm sorry, Alexis," Jasmine said as she walked back to her door and opened it. Just before she stepped in, she turned to me and said, "I'll talk to you later." With that, she went inside and slammed the door.

I stood in the hallway, dumbfounded. Jasmine had showed me her true colors. I guess it is true that blood is thicker than water. And this betrayal was one I'd never forget.

28

Camille

$\mathcal{W}$e had just wrapped up taping on the fourth episode of the show. Talk about excited. We had a Good Girlz meeting yesterday, and Rachel made us talk through the issue of how I got the job. I apologized over and over. I know everybody was salty, especially Alexis. But by the end of the meeting, at least they were talking to me.

Once I got things back right with them and got Walter's parents to stop trippin', everything would be perfect in my life. I was loving my job, and can't even begin to describe the rush I felt when the lights went on and I heard the opening music for the show.

A few times I had even gone to the mall, and people actually recognized me. I was in Baker's shopping for shoes, and I heard these two girls over in the corner.

One said, "Hey, isn't that the host of *Teen Talks*?"

The other girl looked at me. I smiled, and she tried to

whisper to her friend, "I think that's her. Oh, my God. Maybe we should get her autograph."

I guess they decided not to after all, because they never approached me for my autograph. But I was still thrilled to death that, one, they recognized me, and two, they wanted to get my autograph. That's when I realized I needed to start practicing my autograph. I didn't want to be like some celebrities who signed their name and you had no clue what it said.

I made my way back to my dressing room at the studio. I passed the newsroom and watched for a few minutes all the people running around like crazy. I heard them saying something about breaking news. I was glad I didn't work in the news department—they always seemed so stressed out. I no longer wanted to be a news reporter. Now I knew I was destined to be the next Oprah.

My smile faded as I looked at the Get Well card lying on my vanity. I wanted to drop it off to Walter, who was still in the hospital, but his parents had arranged it so that I couldn't visit or call to see how he was doing. They were furious with me, and his mom had all but cursed me out when I called. I knew they were upset, which is why I was trying my best to stay away. I was trying to bury myself in my work and school, and so far, it was working. But the minute I stopped, my thoughts went back to Walter.

Shereen stuck her head into my door, interrupting my thoughts.

"Great show today. You got a minute?" she asked.

"Of course," I said. "I was just about to wipe off some of this makeup before I head out. What's up? Come in."

When she opened the door completely, it was her and two of the show's other producers. My heart started beating kind of fast. I was hoping they weren't there to deliver bad news. But the more I thought about it, nothing good could come from a meeting with all of the producers and me. I just hoped they weren't coming to pull the plug on the show or anything like that.

I looked from Shereen to the others, hoping someone would tell me what this was about. I didn't want to lose my job, especially since it was just getting off the ground.

Shereen started talking first. "Camille, we think you're doing a fantastic job," she started.

Then why are you guys ganging up on me in my dressing room? I wanted to shout. But I kept my mouth closed and waited patiently.

"But we were talking to Ray Williams, the station's general manager, and he, well, we all decided we need more hard-hitting topics. The hottest hairstyles were funny and cute—" Shereen said.

"So was the topic on things to do for summer vacation—" another producer added.

Shereen looked at me. "But we were thinking you could tackle issues that are real and current for teens today. I mean, the purpose of this show is to talk about what you all are going through on a daily basis. Things that bother you, obstacles you've had to overcome, hot topics."

"I have an idea I was thinking about, but I didn't know if it would be too risky for the show," I offered. Honestly, I thought the topics were just fine. I had fun with the hairstyles and the summer break guests. But I didn't want them to take my show away from me, so I was grasping at straws.

"Oh?" Shereen's eyebrows shot up.

"It's a story about a group of girls who steal clothes and stuff from the mall, then resell them to their friends."

Shereen looked at her coworkers. Their eyes lit up right away.

"Teenage boosters, huh?" one producer said.

I shrugged. "It was just an idea I had. I know some girls who used to do it."

"Yeah?" the other producer said, sitting on the edge of her seat.

"It was my friends who were running the business, so I mean I know what it was like, firsthand."

"What?" Shereen cried. "You're kidding me? You've been sitting on this idea all this time?" She broke into a huge smile.

"Well, I didn't know if it was something you guys would let me do," I said, shocked at how excited they were.

"Camille, that's the kind of stuff we want. Stories like that—real issues, stuff that happens with you and your friends. Stories people will be talking about the next day. We want this show to be a true reflection of what teens face today, the temptations, the struggles between doing what's good and bad." Shereen eased back onto the chair. "What else you got?" she asked.

"Well, let me think. Oh, a friend of mine started going out with another friend's brother, and that caused all kinds of issues with their friendship, especially when the brother dumped her."

One of the producers clapped. "See, that's the kind of stuff we're looking for."

"Then another friend stole a research paper, and—"

"Oh, my God! Stolen papers, back-stabbers. That's what I'm talking about," the other producer said. "You think you can get them to come on the show?"

I nodded. I knew I'd have to lie to get them here, but I didn't have a choice.

Shereen looked at me. "I'm glad we chose you, I knew you had it in you. That's the stuff we're looking for, things that you discuss with your friends, situations you find yourselves in and how you get out of them."

They stood. "I'm glad we've had this chance to talk," Shereen said.

"Me too," I offered weakly. I had just thrown out ideas, not really expecting them to use them. I knew none of my girls would be down for going on TV and telling all their business. My gut told me they weren't going to be happy about me using this stuff. I just prayed that as my friends, they'd at least give me a chance. But seeing as how they'd barely forgiven me for how I'd gotten the job in the first place, I just didn't know if this was something they'd ever understand.

29

Alexis

I was so excited about watching Camille do her live taping of *Teen Talks* today.

She'd sat us all down and apologized about how she got the job. She begged us to forgive her and asked us all to come as her special guests to today's show. I was still a little peeved about what she did, but I decided to just let bygones be bygones. I was just really glad that Camille was working to keep our friendship going strong. With all the press coverage and popularity she was getting, I have to admit, in the back of my mind, I wondered if it would go to her head. I was happy to see it hadn't.

"Is this where we're supposed to sit?" I pointed to the first row.

"Yeah, that producer said since we're her friends, we get front-row seats," Angel responded.

"Man, this is cool," Jasmine said as we sat down.

I looked around the small TV studio. There was a crowd

of about thirty teenagers. I recognized a few people from around the area, but for the most part, I had never seen most of the people here.

Camille was actually doing her first live show. She said the others were taped, so this was a big deal. But she was such a natural, I knew she'd do fine.

"Okay, everyone stand by. We're on in five minutes," some short, stocky man came out and shouted.

I felt myself getting all excited, especially when I saw my girl come out onstage. She saw us and waved, and we all eagerly waved back.

"You all know her?" some girl behind us leaned in and asked.

"Yeah, we're best friends," Angel proudly responded.

"Wow, that is so cool," the girl said.

We smiled as we turned back and watched the makeup artist dab Camille's face. I was so happy to see her on that stage. At that very moment I was really happy that she was the one who had gotten the job, however she'd gotten it. She wanted it a lot more than I did, and she was probably a whole lot better than I ever would've been.

The lights in the studio dimmed, and music started playing, I assumed that meant the show was about to start.

We all leaned back and watched Camille get into her zone, which she was really good at.

The director gave a countdown, and Camille took off.

"What's up, everybody? This is your girl Camille Harris

with another edition of *Teen Talks*, and today's show is going to be hot, hot, hot! So kick your shoes off and get ready for a show that everybody will be talking about tomorrow."

I looked at Jasmine and smiled. Even she had a proud look on her face.

"Well, let's not waste any time," Camille continued. "Today we're talking about something you rarely hear about—teenage boosters. That's right, teens who steal, everything from clothes to electronics. But we're taking this discussion one step further by talking about teens who then turn right around and sell the stuff, raking in big bucks. It's the new thing to do, but as some teens are finding out, there's a huge price to pay."

The audience seemed on the edge of their seats. Me, Jasmine, and Angel were in shock, too.

"I know she is not doing this," I hissed.

Jasmine stared straight ahead, stunned.

"Take a look at our TV monitors," Camille continued, pointing to a big screen in the corner. Up popped a mug shot of our friend Trina King, a former Good Girlz member. She was the one who had gotten us caught up in the whole boosting scheme.

"Seventeen-year-old Trina King is doing hard time for her boosting business," Camille continued. Trina would die if she knew that picture was on TV. Her head was cocked to the side. Her hair was all over her head, and of course

she was wearing a frown. She looked like a hard-core crimi-
nal. "As you can see," Camille said. "Trina was arrested and
charged with multiple counts of theft. She was charged as
an adult. Now, for the next twenty-two years, she'll spend
her days on lockdown. No prom. No dates. No gradua-
tion. And for what? Some free Baby Phat T-shirts?"

The audience started mumbling and shaking their
heads.

"I know. Pretty sad, huh?" Camille said as she started
moving toward the audience. The camera followed her.
"With us today we have some other teens who were caught
up in that same boosting ring that sent Trina to jail."

I almost died when Camille walked over to us, and the
camera moved to capture me, Angel, and Jasmine. All three
of us still looked like we were in shock.

I absolutely could not believe Camille was doing this
to us.

"Now, let me be clear. These teens have paid their debt
to society." She pointed to us. "They got off easy, so we're
hoping they'll share their stories with us," Camille said.
"Alexis, you were best friends with Trina. Both of you are
from very rich families. Maybe you can shed some light
on why someone would do this, especially someone who
doesn't have to."

Camille moved the microphone into my face. Every eye
in the audience was on me.

"I, umm, I . . . ," I couldn't get any words out. I think

if I had been in my right mind, I would've gone off, but I was still too shocked to say anything.

Camille moved the microphone back to her mouth. "I understand since you never actually took anything and were only responsible for selling the stuff, you didn't think you did anything wrong."

"Well . . . I mean, at the time . . . I, ummm . . . I guess I just thought, I don't know, that it was no big deal," I struggled to say.

"No big deal?" Camille said, snatching the microphone away. "Ask Trina is it a big deal." She dramatically pointed to a monitor before turning to Angel.

"And Angel, you are a single, unwed teenage mother. Did you take part as a way to feed your child?" Camille said.

Angel's chest started heaving up and down. She had asthma, and the way her breathing started sounding heavy, I was worried that she was about to have an attack. She'd kept her asthma at bay lately, but if this didn't set an attack off, I don't know what would.

"Leave her alone!" Jasmine snapped. She jumped up and glared at Camille.

Camille looked at Jasmine and tried to give her an innocent look. "What? We're just trying to get to the bottom of the motivation behind boosting." Camille looked out the corner of her eye and saw the director giving her some kind of hand signal. She nodded and smiled toward the camera. "Didn't I tell you this show was going to be hot? But we gotta pay the bills, so we have to take a break. But you'd better believe we'll be right back. Stay with us." The music came up as the show went to commercial break.

As soon as the red light went off, Camille leaned in to us and whispered, "Guys, please, please don't be mad. This is just TV, you know, trying to hype stuff up."

I reached out and took Jasmine's arm, because I could tell she was about to haul off and knock the mess out of Camille.

"Camille, how could you do this?" I cried as I stepped in front of Jasmine. "Look at Angel." I pointed to Angel, who had her hand to her chest and was still trying to catch her breath.

"Come on, y'all. I thought you all would understand," she said. "You know I didn't mean anything."

"Whatever, Camille. You knew exactly what you were doing," Jasmine growled.

"And then how you gon' put Trina on front street like that?" I added.

"Trina's mug shot is a matter of public record," Camille said matter-of-factly.

"I thought Tameka was lowdown," Jasmine said, finally calming down herself. "But you, you take the cake."

"Guys," Camille whispered, turning her back to the rest of the audience. "Don't be like that. I mean, part of how we learn from our mistakes is by helping others not make the same mistakes."

"I didn't you see you telling anybody you were buying

some of the stolen merchandise, too," Jasmine snapped.

Camille let out a long breath. "I'm not a part of the story."

Just then, a producer walked over. "Camille, this show is off the chain! Do you teens still say off the chain?" He laughed. "Man, I'm so glad you suggested this. This has to be the best one ever!" He patted her back before racing off.

"So this was all your idea?" I asked, still thinking this was all going to be a bad dream.

"Camille, please tell us this is all a big misunderstanding," Angel said, finally catching her breath.

"I was scared they were gonna pull the show. I had to do something to spice it up. They wanted me to make it hotter," she said.

"So you decided to use your friends to do it," Jasmine said.

"I was hoping you'd understand." Camille lowered her head.

"Fat chance," Jasmine said.

"Yeah." I reached down and grabbed my purse. "I hope this stupid show was worth it."

"Yeah, Miss Superstar," Jasmine added. "You got your hot show. And you just lost three friends."

I waved for Angel to come on, and all three of us made our way out the studio, ignoring the producer who was running after us, begging us not to leave.

30

Alexis

*N*one of us said a word. We had gathered nearly thirty minutes before our scheduled meeting time to talk about how we were going to handle Camille. Nobody had talked to her since the show yesterday. I think we were all too mad.

Angel looked at me and said, "I never in a million years would have thought Camille would do something like that."

I was so mad I still couldn't talk. I just didn't want to believe that Camille used our stories on her show like that.

"How come she didn't do one on helping your fugitive boyfriend hide from the law?" Jasmine said. Everyone chuckled at that.

"Yeah, or what about the current boyfriend being jumped by the ex and his friend?" I added.

Jasmine shook her head in disgust. "I just can't believe

she'd sell us out like that. First Tameka, now Camille. I tell you, with friends like these, who needs enemies?"

I looked at Jasmine. She was one to talk. After the way she did me for Tranita, she was just as guilty. I'd tried to put that whole situation behind me when we went to Camille's show, but shoot, since I was mad, I might as well be mad about everything.

We sat silently for a few minutes. No one said anything until the door creaked open and Tameka came sulking in. No one had forgiven her for stealing Jasmine's research paper. We had all stopped talking to her, unless it was absolutely necessary. Rachel made her apologize to the group. She still denied that she took the paper, but she did apologize for her dirty tricks. We still didn't trust her, and I think she knew there was no way she'd win her way back into our good graces.

"Hey, guys," she said. "I saw the show. That's messed up, what Camille did."

When no one responded, she plopped in a chair, pulled out some book called *Simply Divine*, and buried her face in it.

"So what are we gonna do?" I asked, eyeing the clock. We knew Rachel would be in soon. And we had to wrap it up, because she would only find a way to make a lesson out of all of this. Not to mention, she'd also force us to forgive Camille and try to salvage our friendship. But judging by the look on everyone's face, I had a feeling that was the very last thing on anyone's mind.

Me personally, I wanted to know why she did it in the first place. I mean, why would she use stuff that happened to us, knowing the pain and torture we've been through, then broadcast it for all of Houston to see? I just wanted her to answer that one question, then after that, I never cared if I saw her ever again.

Angel motioned toward the back of the room. "I think under the circumstances, we should pick this conversation up at a later time. Maybe after the meeting we could all go get something to eat, then talk about what our next move should be," she said.

"Oh, so now y'all don't even want to talk around me?" Tameka asked, looking up from her book.

"I thought you were busy reading," I said. She sucked her teeth and turned her attention back to the book.

By the time Rachel entered the room, we had all decided we'd pick up the conversation later at dinner. Rachel walked to the front of the room after saying hello to us.

"Ladies, we have some issues we need to work out," she started.

We looked at each other and smirked. If only she knew.

"Before we get started, I have something to say." Everyone turned to the back of the room. Tameka closed her book and stood up.

"This is my last meeting. I no longer feel welcome here, and I just wanted you guys to know I'm moving on," she said.

I gave her a look like I hope she didn't think someone was going to beg her to stay. Shoot, she was just lucky we'd gotten busy and hadn't gotten around to paying her back for her dirty tricks.

"Tameka," Rachel finally said, "are you sure about this? We'd hate to see you go."

Tameka looked at us, then back at Rachel. "You're probably the only person in here who would hate to see me go. I believe that everyone else can't wait for me to leave."

Rachel looked at us like she wanted us to say something. I, for one, was not about to fake the funk. I could care less if Tameka left.

"Well, I'd like you to give it some more thought," Rachel said.

Angel folded her arms, and Jasmine rolled her eyes. I just sat there quietly, waiting for the girl to pick up her stuff and leave. No point in threatening to leave and you still standing there waiting for someone to beg you to stay.

"Girls, don't you think Tameka should reconsider leaving?" Rachel asked. I'm sure she was sorry she even asked, because the room was so quiet, you could probably hear a pin drop.

Tameka bit her lips as her eyes filled with water. "Auntie, I'm gonna call my mom in your office to come get me."

"Are you sure about this, Tameka?"

Tameka nodded.

"Do you want me to come with you?" Rachel asked.

Tameka shook her head, shot us one last pitiful look, then left the room.

Rachel turned to us sadly. "What is going on with you guys? That was so rude. And your attitudes stink. Is this about the show?"

"So you saw it, too?" I said.

"Actually, I didn't, but Shereen told me all about it. And I talked to Camille. She feels really bad."

"She should," I said.

"And she don't feel too bad, seeing as how she ain't here," Jasmine added.

"She's not here because she couldn't bear to face you all," Rachel said.

"That was very smart," Jasmine growled. "Camille ain't no real friend."

My anger at Camille was starting to shift. With Jasmine sitting over there acting all holy, I was getting mad at her all over again. Finally, I said, "No, you didn't talk about somebody being a real friend."

"Excuse me?" Jasmine sat up in her seat.

"You heard me," I replied. "You sold me out, too. For Tranita. You coulda let me know what was going on."

Jasmine scooted to the edge of her chair. I could tell I had really made her mad. "I tried to tell you from jump.

But no, you all big and bad, saying 'me and Jaquan gon' be together whether you like it or not.' So don't blame me if you got played." She flicked her hand at me and rolled her eyes.

"You still coulda told me." I folded my arms. "I was supposed to be your friend."

"And Jaquan is my brother."

Rachel rubbed her head like she had a serious headache. "Please, would you all stop it? What has happened to you guys? You've turned into people I don't even know. What about forgiveness? You all made some mistakes, why can't we forgive each other and move forward."

"I ain't did nothing," Jasmine snapped, leaning back in her seat. "You need to be talking to the lying, back-stabbing, sell-out other girls."

Rachel sighed. "How can we fix this?" She looked at each of us. No one said anything.

Finally, I said, "We can't." It hurt, but I meant that from the bottom of my heart. As far as I was concerned, my friendships with the Good Girlz had come to an end.

31

Camille

I waited until I heard the phone ringing. When the heavy-set nurse picked up the phone, I walked quickly past the nurses' station and slid into room 321 at the Sugar Land Methodist Hospital. I used the balloon bouquet to shield my face.

Once I was inside, I suddenly regretted my great plan to get in and see Walter. He was sitting up in bed. His mother was standing over him, fussing with the sheets that covered his body.

"I'm so glad you'll be getting out of here, sweetheart," she said.

When Walter looked up at me, he smiled. "Camille," he said.

His mother immediately turned toward me. "How did you get in here?" she snapped. She leaned over to try and get the nurse's call button. "Walter, we need security in here this instant."

Walter pushed the button out of his mother's reach. "Don't do that," he said.

His mother tightened her lips and shot him an evil look. "I want her tossed out. She's the reason you've been in here for nearly three weeks."

"Mom, please don't. I need to talk to her. I haven't seen her in a long time," Walter said.

I finally felt good about my decision to sneak into the hospital to see him. I'd been thinking about it for quite a few days, but I was afraid because I knew his parents were furious with me. Finally, I decided to take my chances because I was missing him so bad.

"Come in, Camille," Walter said. "Thanks for the balloons." I couldn't move from my spot at the door. I didn't want to be anywhere near his mother, especially since she had a look like she wanted to kill me. And looking at Walter in that hospital bed, I can't say that I really blamed her. The color had returned to his cheeks, but there were still dark circles around his eyes, and his chest was all bandaged up. His bottom lip had stitches across it, and his arm was in a cast.

"Mom, just give me a minute, please," he said.

She sighed. "Fine." She grabbed her purse and tossed me a disgusted look. "I'm going to the cafeteria. When I get back, I want her gone. You remember what we talked about, son," she said to Walter before kissing his cheek and rushing by me to get out of the room.

I slowly walked in. I placed the balloons next to the

cards and flowers on the windowsill. Then I walked over to his bed, not knowing quite what to say to him. It was my fault he was in here, and I couldn't say sorry enough.

"Stop looking at me like that," he finally said, with his dimples showing and melting my heart at the same time. "I'm sure I look worse than I feel. I'm going home tomorrow."

I was glad I had gotten to see him now, because once he got home, it was probably going to be next to impossible.

"I've missed you, and I'm so sorry," I said as my eyes filled with tears. "I'm so sorry about what happened to you." I reached down to hug him. He flinched in pain, so I backed off.

"It wasn't your fault, Camille. Really, I don't blame you. I just want them to arrest Keith and his cousin, and I'll be okay."

I couldn't believe he wasn't mad at me.

"You can sit down," he said, using his hand to motion to the chair next to the bed. "We need to talk anyway," he added.

The lump in my throat wouldn't go away. And although I tried, I couldn't seem to calm my heart.

"I've had so much time to think things through in here," he said.

I pulled the chair closer to his bed and leaned in to him. I wanted to take his hand, but the look on his face stopped me cold.

"Camille, you're one of the sweetest, prettiest girls I've ever known, and I really like you a lot. I mean, I could see us together for a long time," he said.

"Oh, Walter, I'm so glad to hear that," I said, breathing a sigh of relief. "I thought for sure this was going to be the end of us."

"Wait, let me finish," he said, holding his hand up to stop me. "I like you a lot, but I really think we should just be friends," he slowly continued. "I think my mom was right about not needing anything to help me lose focus."

His words knocked me back against the chair. They crushed my heart and made me wonder if I should've come in the first place. Had I stayed away, he wouldn't be breaking up with me.

"It's not you, or anything. I just really need to start thinking about school and getting ready for Princeton. This could've really messed up my chances," Walter said.

"But you said you weren't mad at me."

"I'm not. I just . . . I don't know . . . I just promised my mother . . . ."

I didn't know what to say. I was desperately trying to fight back tears as I sat there and listened to him tell me all the reasons why we should just be friends instead of boyfriend and girlfriend.

What could I say? If I were him, I wouldn't want me either. Despite all that stuff about me being nice, the truth was, he had spent weeks in the hospital because of my stupid ex-boyfriend and me. Even if he did want to give me a chance, I'm sure after this, his mother was more adamant than ever about him not seeing me, and I couldn't blame her.

When the nurse came in to check on him, I eased out of the room without saying good-bye. I waited until I left the parking lot to start crying. I had to pull over to the side of the road, I was crying so hard.

The really sad part of all of this was, I couldn't call anyone to talk to. Jasmine, Angel, and Alexis had made it very clear that I was no longer welcome in the group or their lives.

I couldn't remember a time when I felt more alone.

32

Alexis

It wasn't that I didn't like them anymore. We had just grown apart. That's what I told myself as I sat in the back of the room, waiting for Rachel to finish talking to us.

I saw Camille at the store the other day, and I turned and went the other way. And after the way Jasmine played me with Jaquan, I didn't have a whole lot to say to her either.

And although Angel had sided with Jasmine, I really didn't have a beef with her. But honestly, she is so wrapped up in her baby, we didn't talk much anyway. Now it looked like none of us were talking. We just seemed to be drifting apart. It almost seemed like Camille was the glue holding us all together, and now that she was gone, we were falling apart.

After that disaster of a talk show, she'd called all three of us, apologizing again. And although her apology sounded really sincere, I still wasn't trying to hear it. Everybody and their mama saw that show, and if they didn't, they'd heard about it. My mom had even heard about it, and she had almost lost her mind that I would get on TV and embarrass her like that. I mean, even Angel was through with Camille. Jasmine went off on her every time she called.

I was just about to stand up to leave when I looked up to see Camille standing in the doorway. She looked like she was unsure whether she should come in. I hoped she wasn't trying to get the okay from me.

"Hello, Camille," Rachel said when she noticed her standing there. "Come on in."

I know me and Jasmine rolled our eyes as she walked in. She sat down in the front row, which was empty.

"Camille, do you have something you'd like to say?" Rachel asked.

"I just wanted to tell everyone I'm sorry," she replied.

"I have to agree with that," Jasmine snarled.

"Jasmine!" Rachel snapped.

"No, Miss Rachel," I jumped in. "Jasmine's right. Camille was always the one talking about playing fair and square. She's such a hypocrite."

"I am not," Camille softly protested.

"I don't know what you call it, then," Angel said. "You were so wrong for what you did."

"You guys don't understand. I was under a lot of pressure," Camille said. She looked like she desperately wanted us to believe her.

"I don't care what kind of pressure you're under. You don't sell out your friends," Jasmine said.

"And you don't stab them in the back," I added.

"I didn't stab you in the back. They told me I probably would've won anyway."

We all looked at her like she was so full of it.

"But we'll never know now, will we?" I asked. "Obviously you didn't have enough faith that you'd get it without cheating. But hey, you got what's most important to you—your show."

"I wouldn't expect you to understand," Camille told me. "You didn't even need the money."

"*And?* Maybe I wanted the job for reasons other than money. Maybe I wanted to feel good about something I was doing. But I'll never know now because I chose not to cheat my way into the job." I was tired of listening to Camille's lame apologies. I stood up and said, "I'm about to go."

"Alexis, sit down," Rachel commanded.

I huffed, but sat back down. Rachel took a deep breath before she started talking about how much all of this was hurting her. By the time Rachel finished her speech about how heartbreaking it was for her to see us this way, all four of us looked like we were fighting back tears, but they were tears of anger more than anything else.

"You guys have done such wonderful things together. If I had any idea this teen show was going to be the end of all our hard work, I would've simply told Shereen to find someone else," Rachel said, looking like she wanted to cry herself.

I couldn't wait to get out of there, I was getting tired of listening to Rachel go on and on about how we could've made such a difference and so forth. Finally, when I couldn't take it anymore, I stood up again.

"Miss Rachel, thanks for everything you did for us. I really appreciate you helping us out and showing us a better way. But honestly, I think that everyone just got caught up in doing their own thing. I don't think it's really anything too personal. We all love you, and we'll even help out if you need help with the kids, but I just think it's time we all move on," I said.

Rachel stared at me a moment, then said, "How many of you feel that way?" Everyone raised their hands.

Rachel let out a long sigh. "I understand, Alexis. Just know that you can still call me anytime you need to talk or whenever you need anything."

I waved good-bye and left before I started crying. I stood out front for a few minutes, contemplating going back inside to tell everyone, Let's just make up. But each time I thought about it, I changed my mind. There was no point in me forcing myself onto anyone, especially with them turning out to be friends like they'd proven themselves to be.

Jaquan pulled up as I was walking to my car. Could

this day get any worse? I thought as I looked over in his passenger seat. There was a girl with long, golden brown braids and a huge chest, sitting there, a big cheesy grin on her face.

Jaquan was smiling, too. Until he saw me. His smile faded, and I saw him rolling down his window to say something. I took off to my car before he could see me burst out in tears.

33

Alexis

I was too through. My parents had gone from arguing in the same house to arguing over the phone. Earlier today, I'd spent over an hour eavesdropping on their phone conversation. I know it was wrong, but I heard my mom telling a friend that she and my dad had gone to a marriage counselor after he moved out. So, that had me thinking there was hope that they would work all of this out. That is, until I heard them on the phone, biting each other's heads off.

They both blamed each other for the downfall of their marriage. At first, I was thinking maybe the counseling would help them, but after hearing them on the phone, I doubted it very seriously.

I was so disgusted after overhearing my parents, that I'd called two of my old friends to go out with.

I hadn't talked to Angel, Jasmine, or Camille in two weeks. I was trying to forget my troubles and move on with my life. That's why I'd agreed to go out tonight to Club Coco Loco with Mari and Marlee.

Mari and Marlee were twins. They were brown-skinned, tall, with long hair, and had bodies like models. So needless to say, going out with them meant instant attention, not to mention, most of the time, easy access into the VIP lounges. The problem was you had to be eighteen to get in to Coco Loco. But both of them assured me that they had it covered.

Mari prepared to turn her keys over to the valet, and we stepped out of the car like princesses. I was shocked when she slipped me a fake ID for someone named Jaimi Huff, who looked incredibly like me.

Even the VIP line was snaked around the corner, but the wait was quite entertaining, since Mari and Marlee knew just about everyone in Houston. We didn't have to wait long, anyway, because the VIP line moved quickly.

"Wanna go to the VIP lounge first?" Mari asked me.

"Sure, let's do this," I answered. I was already feeling the music, and we hadn't been in there a good five minutes. I wanted to get my party on, but I figured we'd go check out the lounge first.

"Girl, I told you, this place was tight," Mari bragged in my ear as we looked around the room.

We made our way through the crowded club, stopping in the bathroom, which was jam-packed as well. But I didn't mind—the music was thumping, and I was so ready to get my groove on.

At the entrance to the VIP lounge, a man wider than all three of our bodies put together stepped in front of us. He had a permanent frown across his face. I was getting ready to turn around and head back toward the dance floor, but Marlee eased up to him with confidence.

"What's up, girls." He smiled as he realized who they were. He stepped aside and let us in after he checked our names off the list.

"Now let's really get this party started," Mari yelled as she led us into the VIP lounge. In there, the music wasn't as loud, but people were dancing. Some were sitting at tables talking, and others were in dark corners, all up under somebody.

I looked around the room to try and scope out a spot for us, but Mari seemed to have everything under control. We parked at a table, and soon the drinks started flowing. I didn't really drink and wasn't sure I was ready to then, but I didn't want to seem out of place. I ordered some wine, thinking that wouldn't be too strong.

After about an hour or so of drinking, dancing, and having a really good time, Mari motioned me closer with her finger.

"You having a good time?" she asked.

"Yeah, girl. I need to hang out with y'all more often." I laughed.

"Good. I was just looking out for you, making sure everything's cool," she said.

"Well, yeah, then, I'm good to go," I said.

When a couple got up from a dark corner in the room, Mari made a beeline for their table. "C'mon over here, Alexis," she said over her shoulder.

Marlee, who was out on the dance floor, noticed us moving, and she walked right off, leaving the guy looking clueless. When we got over to the corner, Mari dug into her purse and pulled out a freezer bag half full of pills.

At first I didn't react or anything, just kept swaying to the music and singing along with Lil Jon & the Eastside Boyz.

"What's up, Alexis?" Marlee giggled.

"Nothing, I'm cool." The truth was, I was starting to feel a bit light-headed from the wine. I wasn't used to drinking, and I probably should've slowed my roll a bit. And the sight of those pills definitely had me nervous.

"You okay, girl?" Mari asked.

"Yeah, I'm straight, I keep telling y'all," I said.

"Well, why don't you have one of these?" She opened her hand, revealing a little blue pill in her palm.

"What's that?" I asked, knowing full well that was Ecstasy.

"A lil' sumptin' sumptin' to make your troubles go away," Marlee answered.

I didn't know a whole lot about drugs, but I did know enough to just say no. "Naw, I'm straight," I said.

"Girl, you think you having a good time now? Wait

until you get this in you. Baby, you ain't ever partied like this before," Marlee assured me.

"Naw, I'ma pass."

Mari snatched a glass of something from another table. "Party pooper," she said as she popped the pill in her mouth. She handed one to her sister, who popped a pill in her mouth as well.

Mari rolled her eyes at me as she jumped up and bounced onto the dance floor. Marlee followed her, leaving me standing off to the side, looking lost.

I sat there for a few minutes looking around the club. What was I doing here? This wasn't even my scene. I missed my girls, and as much fun as I was trying to tell myself I was having, this just wasn't cutting it.

The music was loud, and people were all over each other. Mari finally walked back over to me. She was sweating like crazy and walking like she was about to fall over.

"Alexis . . . ," she said, reaching for my arm. "Call . . . for . . . help. I . . . can't breathe. Wh—where's Marlee?"

Before I could respond, Mari collapsed to the floor. I stood there, stunned as several people started screaming.

34

Camille

"Angel, please stop crying, I can't understand a word you're saying. Please, tell me what happened."

I was sleeping in Saturday morning when the ringing phone woke me up. I wondered why my mom didn't get it, but realized it was seven-thirty in the morning, and she left for work at six.

"Now who is in the hospital, and what happened?" I asked, trying to wipe the sleep from my eyes. Angel was crying so hard I could barely understand her. But since I hadn't talked to her in almost three weeks, I knew this had to be major. "Calm down before you have an asthma attack. And tell me what's going on."

"It's Alexis," Angel said, trying to catch her breath. "She overdosed. We all need to go to the hospital. You've got to come. Camille, I don't care what problems we have with each other, we need to support her."

"Overdose? Since when did Alexis start taking drugs?"

I screamed into the phone as I jumped up from my bed. I know I hadn't seen or talked to any of the Good Girlz lately, but dang, drugs? That didn't even make sense.

"You know Tilly, from school?"

"Yeah, what about her?" I said.

"She called me this morning and said she was at Coco Loco last night when she saw Alexis overdose. She said they rushed her to the hospital and everything. Tilly asked the bouncer, and he said they took her to Memorial Herman off fifty-nine. She knew we hung out with Alexis, so she called me. I tried to call Alexis's mom, but I can't get her. Hurry and get there," Angel said, rushing the words out. "My mom is going to drop me off."

I hung up the phone without even saying 'bye. I raced to the shower and said a silent prayer that Alexis was okay. We might not be talking to each other, but I didn't want anything to happen to her. Shoot, I didn't want anything happening to any of them. I still loved them like they were my sisters. My tears mixed with the hot water in the shower as I kept telling myself this must be some kind of mistake. We don't do drugs. I caught myself. There was no "we" anymore.

I was dressed and out the door in ten minutes. I stopped only briefly to leave my mom a note, since I couldn't call her at her job. I then drove like crazy to the hospital, making it in record time

I raced to the emergency room nurse's station. "Excuse

me, I'm looking for an Alexis Lansing," I said, half out of breath.

"You and everybody else," the nurse said, shaking her head. She pointed over to the waiting area. Angel, Jasmine, Rachel, Angel's mother, and even Tameka were standing in a small circle, talking. I immediately feared the worst.

"What's going on?" I asked as I made my way over to them. "Is Alexis going to be all right?"

Rachel must've sensed the fear I felt because she immediately took my hand. I jerked my hand away. "Alexis is all right, right?"

Rachel shook her head. "No, no. It looks like there's been some misunderstanding."

I looked at Angel. Rachel wasn't making sense.

Angel wrung her hands together. "It wasn't Alexis who overdosed."

"Well, who was it, then?" I said, looking to Rachel for answers.

Jasmine was the one who answered. "She started hanging back out with those uppity girls from her school. It was one of them."

"Alexis and her mother were gone by the time we arrived, but Mari's mother—that's the girl Alexis was with—explained everything," Rachel added.

"Was Alexis doing drugs?" Tameka asked. We all looked at her as if to say, What was she doing here anyway?

"What?" Tameka said, shooting us a look back. "So I can't be concerned about Alexis?"

"We thought you weren't concerned with anyone but yourself," Jasmine snapped.

"I didn't come here for you—" Tameka began.

Rachel immediately cut them off. "Don't you two start. Jasmine, are you Alexis's friend?"

Jasmine looked at Rachel like that was a dumb question. "Well, yeah."

"Hmmph, I can't tell," Rachel said. "I seem to recall you breaking off your friendship with her. So the way I see it, Tameka has just as much right to be here as you do."

I waited for a triumphant look to cross Tameka's face. I was shocked when it didn't.

"I'm assuming Alexis was fine, since the nurse said she and her mother left about twenty minutes ago," Rachel continued. "But I have a suggestion." She dug in her purse and pulled out her cell phone. "How about you call her and find out." She handed me the phone. I just stared at it and didn't take it. She moved it toward Jasmine, then Angel. Both of them did the same.

Rachel shook her head. "Some friends you guys are."

"I'll call her," Tameka said, stretching her hand out to take the phone.

Don't ask me why, but I was offended. Tameka didn't even like Alexis, so what was she trying to prove by offering to call her?

"Look," Tameka said, noticing the expression on my face. "I don't want to start any mess. I know I did some jacked-up things, but honestly, I like hanging with you guys. And I . . . I don't know. I just want to make sure Alexis is fine."

I think all of us were shocked by Tameka's change of heart. I don't know if we could get used to the new Tameka, not that we'd have to, anyway, since none of us were talking.

"Well, *mija,* since we know your friend is fine, we'd better get going," Angel's mother said. Angel looked at us like she wanted to say something. Instead she just nodded to her mother.

"Good-bye, everyone," Angel's mom said as she walked off.

Angel waved when she reached the door. "Bye, y'all."

I wanted to stop her. This was our chance to make up. So why wouldn't any words come out of my mouth? Probably because I knew everyone was still mad at me, and I didn't want my efforts to make up thrown up in my face again.

I looked back at Jasmine, who had turned her attention somewhere else like she was still mad.

Rachel shook her head in disgust. "I'm going to check on Mari. Her mother and sister are distraught, and I want to pray with the family before I go. Tameka, do you need to ride home with me?"

"No, I have my mom's car."

"Fine." Rachel looked at us like she wanted to say something else. I guess she decided against it, because she just sighed as she left and made her way back down the hallway.

"You know what, y'all something else," Tameka said to me and Jasmine. "You want to put me down for not being a real friend. But the way I see it, neither are you guys."

She shook her head as walked out of the waiting room, leaving me and Jasmine standing there speechless.

35

Alexis

If I wanted any more proof that counseling wasn't working, I had it.

My parents were standing in our living room, yelling back and forth, trying to figure out who was to blame for my "spiral into the bad girl role."

My mom nearly had a heart attack when she found out what happened to Mari. Why the police had to call her anyway was beyond me. It's not like I did anything wrong. But they called her, then she called my dad and he'd come rushing over. They were totally trippin'. It's not like I took any drugs. My mom had made the hospital run all kinds of tests anyway, and my dad looked like he was about to blow a gasket.

Mari had to stay overnight at the hospital after having her stomach pumped, but thankfully, she was going to be okay. Still, she had us all scared to death. Marlee had totally freaked out all the way to the hospital and wouldn't leave her sister's side. Then the police wanted to question me about where the drugs came from. That was drama I could live without. And what if I had taken that X? It could've been me laid up in the hospital. No thanks.

I plopped down on the sofa, preparing for a lecture I really wasn't in the mood for.

"What are you doing hanging around with girls who do drugs?" my mother said. She and my dad were standing over me in our living room.

I glared at her. "But she's from such a good family, Mother," I said, my voice laced with sarcasm.

My mother threw up her hands in exasperation. "Arthur, would you talk to your daughter? Because I don't know how much more of this smart-mouthing I can take."

My father sat down on the sofa next to me. "Lexi, what is with this attitude . . . this change?"

I sighed. I debated giving my usual "nothing" response, but I decided if my dad wanted to know what was wrong, I was about to tell him. "I hate my life. There, are you happy?"

My father shook his head like that was the craziest thing he'd ever heard. "What are you talking about, Lexi? You have everything you could ever want, and things other people only dream about."

I stood up. "Do I, now? Do I have a family? I don't think so. Do I have a boyfriend? Nope. Do I have best friends? No. I'm all by myself. Nobody cares about me." I know I sounded like a whiny little brat, but I was tired of acting like everything—the divorce, me and Jaquan, and me and my friends—wasn't bothering me.

"Honey, we love you," my dad said, softening his tone.

I rolled my eyes. "Yeah, right. Your idea of love is raising the limit on my credit card. And Mom, when's the last time you put my needs in front of your own? It took the threat of a divorce before you even paid me any attention." I began pacing back and forth across the living room. Since I was on a roll, I was going to let it all out. I was mad at the world, and my parents were about to bear the brunt of my anger.

"You two are the most selfish people in the world. Me and Sharon didn't ask to be brought into this world. And you make me sorry we were."

"Lexi! Don't say stuff like that," my mother said.

"Why? I'm just a burden to you. If I wasn't here, you could each just go your separate ways and forget the other one exists. That's what you want to do, anyway."

My father looked shocked—I guess because I'd never really gone off like I was going off now.

"You know what, I was upset about you two getting a divorce. But I don't care! I hate this family, and we'd all be better off if we never spoke to one another again."

"Alexis, stop being dramatic," my mother said.

"Huh?" I looked at my mother like she'd lost her mind. "Isn't that the pot calling the kettle black?"

"Alexis Denise Lansing," my father interrupted. "I understand you're upset, but you will not disrespect your mother."

"Why not? You do. You disrespect your promise to her, to us. You promised God you'd stay together. None of that matters to you. We haven't been a family in years. Think about it. We don't even go to church together anymore. We don't go anywhere together anymore. No wonder our family fell apart." I looked at my mother. "Mama, maybe you should disguise your marriage as a business deal, and I'm sure then Daddy will find a way to make it work."

"Enough!" my father said as he stormed over and stood in my face. "You stop all of this smart-mouthing right now."

I glared at him, determined not to cry. "Or what? You'll lower the balance on my credit cards? You'll trade my BMW for a Nissan?" I swear, for a minute, I thought my dad was going to hit me. But I really didn't care. They both made me sick.

"Where is all of this anger coming from?" my mother said as she gently put her hand on my father's arm and eased him away from me. He moved. I think he was still in shock over my outburst.

My mother looked at me with a concern I hadn't seen in years. "Please tell us what's going on. You're hanging out with the wrong crowd. You're mad at the world. What happened to our sweet little girl?"

"She doesn't exist anymore," I said, finally letting the tears out. "You made sure of that." I know I was probably emotional about everything going on in my life, but I was just sick and tired of everything and everybody.

My parents looked at each other, and for once they both seemed at a loss for words.

"Alexis, please talk to us. Tell us what is going on."

"Just leave me alone, okay. Please." I didn't give them time to say anything else as I took off upstairs to my room.

I threw myself across my bed as I thought about my life. How had everything spiraled into this?

I lay on my bed thinking until I finally dozed off. I had been asleep a couple of hours when I heard a knock on my bedroom door.

My parents stuck their heads in when I didn't answer. "Can we talk to you?" my father said.

"Whatever," I said, rolling over on my back. At this point, I just wanted them to leave me alone and let them go on with their funky little lives.

My father sat down on my bed. My mother sat on the sofa across from my bed. "Sit up and look at us," my father ordered.

I blew a frustrated breath as I sat up. I crossed my arms as I waited for them to talk.

"Alexis, first, let me apologize. On behalf of your mother and I . . . we . . . we want to say, we're sorry," my father began. "I know things haven't been easy on you these last few months. Heck, they haven't been easy on any of us lately."

My mother nervously rubbed her hands together as she jumped in. "Your father and I can't agree on much lately," she added. "But one thing we do agree on is how much we love you. And the fact that we didn't do enough to show you that."

I felt my anger dissolving. It had been so long since I'd seen my parents act civil about anything together.

"Your mother and I also agree that we made a lot of mistakes." He looked up at her. "We've been seeing a counselor. We didn't want you to know because we didn't want you to get your hopes up."

I tried to keep a straight face so I wouldn't let on that I knew already.

"But truthfully," my dad continued. "I don't think either of us gave it a real chance."

My mother nodded in agreement. "But watching you, watching this outburst, and this person you've become, well it's just putting some things back in perspective."

I looked back and forth between the two of them. "What are you saying?"

"We're saying, we haven't been successful with fixing our marriage because nobody wanted to take the blame for it being broken," my father said.

"So you're not getting a divorce?" I asked.

"Sweetie, I don't know what we're going to do," my father said. "But we're going to keep seeing the counselor. We owe it to you and Sharon to at least try."

I turned to my mother. "Is he for real?"

My mother walked over to me. "He is. We are. We've been talking since you came up to your room and we both agree that we never took into account what this was doing to you." She rubbed my hair. "When I think of what could've happened had you been the one taking those drugs, well, fighting with your father seems so trivial. Baby, I know we haven't been the best parents. When I saw what we'd turned my sweet, sweet child into, well, let's just say I didn't like it." She paused and lifted my chin. Tears filled her eyes. "So I'm willing to do whatever I can to bring her back. Because I don't believe you when you say she doesn't exist anymore. Now, don't get me wrong, you mouth off like that again and you're in a world of trouble."

Shoot, I didn't even care about getting in any trouble. My parents weren't getting a divorce, at least not anytime soon.

"I can't promise you it'll be easy." My mother sighed. "I mean, you know I'm a shopaholic, and Macy's is having their three-day sale, so I'm not going to be able to go cold turkey." She smiled. "But I'll try."

My father squeezed her hand. "*We'll* try. And we both recognize our problems are much deeper than your mother's shopping. I neglected you and your mother . . ." He paused.

"And Sharon. I promise I'll try to do better. So we just ask that you be patient with us, with our family."

I jumped up and threw my arms around my father's neck. "Daddy, you just don't know how much this means to me." I squeezed him, then hugged my mother. "Thank you, Mama. You all won't regret it. We can make this work."

I was so happy. Maybe I should've gone off a long time ago. My family was staying together. Now if I could just get my friends to do the same.

"No, thank you, baby," my father said as he took my mother's hand. "For helping us remember what's really important."

My mother smiled, and for the first time in I don't know how long, my parents kissed.

36

Camille

Thoughts of Walter invaded my mind for the millionth time today. I couldn't believe things were over with us just like that. I didn't know that I could really blame him, though. If his ex-girlfriend had put me in the hospital, I'd have to ask myself what I was getting into. Throw in pressure from his parents, and I guess I could understand why he decided to break up with me.

Still, that didn't ease the pain in my heart.

I think what made things even worse for me was that I really didn't have anyone to talk to anymore. I tried to call my old friends Melanie and Tonya, but both of them blew me off. I guess they were still salty because they said I dumped them for the Good Girlz.

I felt a lump form in my throat as I fought back tears and thought about the fact that I had lost three of the best friends I'd ever had. Over the last year, Alexis, Angel, and Jasmine had shown me what true friendship really was. And

I repaid them how? By lying, cheating, and using them. What was wrong with me? I thought as I slapped my head. And why didn't I try to make up when I had the chance?

"Hey, Camille, good show today."

I looked up to see Shereen, who had stuck her head in my dressing room.

"May I come in?" she asked.

I nodded as I checked my reflection in the mirror to make sure my eyes weren't red. Shereen walked in and sat down next to me.

"You wanna talk about it?"

Was it that obvious? "Talk about what?"

"Whatever it is that has caused you to lose your spark." Shereen looked at me with sympathetic eyes.

I definitely didn't want to be whining and crying to my boss. "Naw, I'm fine. Just battling allergies," I said.

She nodded like she knew I was lying. "You know, my grandmother used to always say, 'You shouldn't bear false witness against your neighbor.' That was her favorite commandment."

Now, my mother was a devout Christian, and I was raised in the church, but I didn't pay as much attention in Bible study as I probably should've. "That's the one about lying, right?"

"Yep. It seems like such a little thing, and oftentimes we don't think it's that big of a deal," Shereen said. "But when we do it, especially against people we care about, it's not pleasing in the eyes of God."

I looked at her, and the tears I was holding back finally came out. "I lost them all, all three of my best friends. They hate me," I cried.

"Well, what you did was kind of messed up," she replied matter-of-factly.

I looked at Shereen. "You know what I did?"

She nodded. "Camille, this is my show, and I've always wanted it to succeed, but I would never sacrifice someone I cared about for this." She pointed around the dressing room. "Especially because . . ." Her voice trailed off.

I stared at her, waiting on her to finish. "Especially because what?"

"Especially because television is a fickle business." Shereen let out a long sigh.

"What does that mean?" I asked.

Shereen took a deep breath like it hurt her to say what she was about to tell me. "Camille, they're canceling the show."

"What?" I had to have heard her wrong.

"The show is not doing as well as they thought."

"Huh? That doesn't make sense. Everyone is raving about the show."

Shereen shook her head. "No, everyone raved about the first few episodes, but it's just not pulling in the ratings that they wanted it to. It's no reflection on your talent. It's just, well, it's just the way things go."

I fell back against my chair. Canceled? I'd lost everything for this show, and they were canceling it?

"What did I do wrong?" My voice was just above a whisper, I was in such shock.

"I told you, it wasn't you." Shereen stood up. "Believe me, I'm upset, too. But the bigwigs wanted to cut their losses before it was too late." Shereen reached over and squeezed my shoulder. "You will receive a check for three months, which was how long the original contract for the show ran."

I just stared at her. I didn't remember anything about a contract. I was just so happy to get the job that I signed without reading it, just trusting that Rachel wouldn't let Shereen screw me over. And honestly, right about now, I didn't really care about the money.

"I'm sorry," Shereen said. "You can take your time getting your stuff out of the dressing room."

She stopped right before she walked out. "You know, everything happens for a reason. We don't often understand God's motives, but the things He does or doesn't do for us are ultimately in our best interest."

I wasn't in the mood to hear any spiritual lessons. But I forced a smile.

"Camille?"

"Yeah," I said, still trying not to collapse in tears.

"Call your friends. Make up. Apologize. Just work it

out, because when it all boils down to it, family and friends are the only thing that really matters."

I took in her words as she walked out. I would give anything right now to talk to Alexis, Angel, or Jasmine. Shoot, at this point, I'd even take Tameka.

My vibrating cell phone snapped me out of my thoughts. I picked it up.

"Hey, Camille. It's Rachel. I'm just giving you a reminder call about the talent showcase tomorrow night. I expect to see you there. The girls we mentor expect to see you there, okay? Put aside your differences for one night and come support these young girls."

I definitely was in no mood to go smile and fake it around anybody, but I didn't want to disappoint the girls, who I know had worked so hard for the talent showcase. "Okay. I'll be there," I replied.

Rachel paused. "Wait, that was too easy. What's wrong?"

"Nothing," I softly said. "I'll be there."

Rachel was quiet for a minute. "Okay. And Camille— I'm here if you need to talk to me."

I nodded like she could actually see me before pressing end on my cell phone. *Everything happens for a reason.* Something told me this meeting was my last chance to make things right with my friends, and now, more than anything, I wanted to do just that.

37

Alexis

I stared out the window as I watched my parents sitting out by the pool. They were laughing and talking, something I hadn't seen them do in a very long time.

As happy as I was that they were working things out, something still felt missing in my life. I looked over at the picture of me, Angel, Camille, and Jasmine that was sitting on my dresser. We took that picture at the last community service project. That's what was missing—my girls.

I tried to fill the void I felt when they were gone by hanging out with Mari and Marlee, and look how that almost ended.

I couldn't help but think if me, Camille, Angel, and Jasmine were still friends, still part of the Good Girlz, that whole disaster with the twins would've never happened. But the more I thought about it, the more I realized we all were wrong. Yes, Camille tripped out by telling all of our business. But I was just as guilty too, for putting Jasmine in the spot I did. When things no longer worked out with me and Jaquan, I put Jasmine in the middle, basically making her choose sides. How was I gon' get upset because she chose her brother?

Even though I realized all of that, I didn't quite know how to pull things back to where they had been.

I sighed. Just let it go, I told myself as I gathered up my things to go to the Zion Hill youth talent showcase, where the little girls we mentored were supposed to be performing. I really didn't want to go because I didn't want to see Camille, Angel, and Jasmine, but Rachel had requested that we all be there—plus, I knew how much it meant to the girls.

It took me about twenty minutes to get to the church. I was grateful that I was the first one there. I wished that I could go straight to the sanctuary to avoid having to bump into anyone, because I was sure I would break down. But Rachel had asked us to meet in the conference room.

Within the next five minutes, Angel arrived, followed by Jasmine, then Camille. We all said "Hey," but that was it.

When Rachel walked in, she must've sensed the tension. She took a deep breath.

"Hello, everyone."

We all muttered halfhearted hellos.

Rachel set her Bible down on the rectangular table at the front of the room. "Oh, good grief. This is ridiculous. No one is going to say this, but I will," she said. "We need to figure out the problem and get you girls back together. I don't know why y'all trying to play hard. You can't pretend you all don't care about one another. When you thought Alexis was in the hospital, each and every one of you stopped what you were doing and raced to the hospital."

A confused look crossed my face. "What?"

Rachel crossed her arms and glared at Angel, Camille, and Jasmine. They all looked away. "That's right. They all hightailed it to the hospital because they thought you were the one that had overdosed."

I looked at Camille. "Is that true?"

Camille shrugged and turned her head.

"Of course it's true," Rachel snapped. "I'm not going to sit up here in church and lie to you. All three of them were a nervous wreck."

I stared at all three of the girls; every one looked away.

"Now, enough is enough," Rachel continued. "Before we go out in that sanctuary, I want us to talk about this." Rachel turned to Camille. "We will start with you. You were wrong for betraying your friends by putting all their business out there like that."

Camille lowered her head in shame. "I know, and I'm so sorry. I feel so bad. I was just so desperate to get the job. I wasn't thinking. I know I was wrong." She started playing with her belt strap. "I had made up my mind that I was going to beg for you all to forgive me today. I miss y'all so much. I know I was out of order with the things I did. I just hope one day you guys can forgive me." She sighed. "I deserved for them to cancel the show."

We all gasped at that. As mad as I may have been at Camille, I still knew how much that show meant to her.

"Dang, I'm sorry, Camille," Angel said.

"Don't be," Camille replied. "I was sad at first, but then the more I thought about it, the more I realized it was probably for the best."

"I'm glad they canceled that stupid show," Jasmine snapped.

Everyone looked at her.

"I'm sorry, but I am glad. We were fine before that stupid competition for the show. I'm just glad it's over," Jasmine admitted.

"Yeah, me too," I offered. Since things had turned around for my parents, maybe they could turn around for us as well. I was tired of pretending I didn't care either. I was going to let them know how I felt. "Thank you all for coming to check on me. You all just don't know how much I miss you guys. I'm sorry for what I did, Jasmine. I should've never put you in the middle of me and Jaquan."

"You shouldn't have," she said matter-of-factly. "I tried to tell you my brother loses interest in girls faster than he changes his stinky socks. Shoot, him and Tranita broke up again anyway."

I couldn't help but feel a flutter of happiness at that.

"Guys, I just want us to get back to the way things used

to be," Camille said. "Out of everything, your friendships meant the most. I mean, I lost the show. I lost Walter—"

"You and Walter broke up?" Angel asked.

"Yeah, I guess he gave in to pressure from his parents."

"Yeah, getting your butt kicked by the ex will do that to you," Jasmine said with a laugh.

Rachel smiled at that. I think we all were happy to share a laugh together.

When the room door creaked open, everyone turned around and looked toward it.

Tameka stuck her head in the door. She looked around, panting like she was nearly out of breath. "Oh, I didn't know y'all were in here," she said before stepping fully into the room. She was clutching a plant wrapped in bright tissue paper with a big paper D hanging at the end of a ribbon.

At first no one said a word.

"Um, I was looking for Auntie Rachel," Tameka said nervously.

"Tameka, don't start with that lying," Rachel said. "I told you to come because I wanted you here, too."

I looked at Tameka. She seemed more and more humble each time we saw her.

"Well, I mean . . . I just came because I wanted to bring this to you guys . . . I don't know, as a way to say I'm sorry, I guess," Tameka said.

I almost fell over backward in my chair.

"Y'all don't understand. I never really had any friends, and I guess I just didn't know how to be one either." Tameka tossed her hair out of her eyes. "I know I was a jerk, but I'm asking for another chance to be a member of the Good Girlz."

We all stared at Tameka, I guess wondering what kind of trick she had up her sleeve.

"You know, Tameka, like we talked about, you have to earn trust, so I think over time you can show the girls that you can be a good friend." Rachel turned to us. "And after the mistakes everyone here has made, I'm sure they'll give you another chance."

Tameka looked at us. "I hope so."

I wanted to still be mad at Tameka, but honestly, I didn't even have the energy anymore.

"What's that?" Rachel asked, pointing to the plant in Tameka's arms.

"A peace offering."

Tameka walked over and handed the plant to me. "Here, this is for you guys," she said.

"Ah, Tameka," Jasmine said. "Why is there a big D hanging off that plant?" She read the ribbon. "Rest in Peace, Big D?"

Rachel snapped her head our way. "Is that from Brother Donell's funeral tomorrow?"

Tameka plastered on an innocent look.

"Why y'all always gotta be starting mess?" she said

playfully. "I just thought you guys would like a nice little plant. I mean, it was just sitting out there on the table, so I thought . . ."

"What?" I said. Everyone started laughing. "Girl, how are you gonna be stealing plants from a dead person, at a church?"

We all started laughing as Chelsea, one of the little girls we mentor, poked her head in the door. "Can I come to y'alls party?"

We smiled and motioned for her to come in. She ran over and gave each of us a hug. "You know what?" she said. "When I grow up, I want to have friends just like you guys," she said.

We all smiled.

"We are friends," I said.

"To the end," Camille added.

"Oh, my God, please don't start that corny stuff," Jasmine said, rolling her eyes.

"Does that include me?" Tameka asked, a serious look across her face.

I looked at my girls. They nodded. "Why not?" I said, as I reached out for her hand.

Rachel had tears in her eyes. "You guys make me so happy."

"Well, you know what would make me happy?" Chelsea said. "If I can get a dollar to go buy some candy. Some girl is selling it out at choir rehearsal."

Rachel smiled as she handed Chelsea a dollar. "Here, then, go get in place for the talent showcase. We'll be out in a minute."

"Thank you, Miss Rachel." Chelsea grabbed the money, then scurried off.

Rachel turned back to us. "You girls have come a long way over this past year. And I'm just proud to have been along for the ride."

I reached over and took Jasmine's hand. "The ride isn't over. It's just beginning."

"And with friends like these," Camille added, "we can't help but be friends for life."

"I wouldn't want it any other way," Angel added.

We all looked at Jasmine. "Excuse me while I go throw up, because you guys have got to be the mushiest, corniest people I've ever met."

"But you love us." Camille draped her arm through Jasmine's.

Jasmine cut her eyes. "Okay, fine. I'll give you all that. I love y'all, corny butts and all."

"Me too?" Tameka grinned widely.

Jasmine stared at her. "One step at a time. One step at a time."

We all cracked up laughing, happy because the Good Girlz, plus one, were finally back in business.

Reading Group Guide

A Conversation with ReShonda Tate Billingsley

Q: *With Friends Like These* is the third book in your series of Christian teen novels, each having one of the Ten Commandments as its theme. With honesty being the theme of this book what do you think is the greatest benefit of telling the truth? When, if ever, do you consider it appropriate to lie?

A: As much as we may try to justify it, I don't think there's ever an appropriate time to lie. That's because one lie leads to another, then another, and so on. Often, people will tell lies to avoid hurting someone's feelings; eventually, that person ends up hurt anyway, and a lie only compounds that hurt.

Q: What advice would you give parents about how to have an honest rapport with their children? How can they have a relationship based on truth with their teens while still respecting their privacy?

A: While I'm not one of those parents who believe you must be your child's friend, I still do think there is a certain level of respect that should be extended to your child. By showing your child you respect him or her as an individual, you're teaching him or her to respect you. That, in turn, helps build a desire to be truthful.

Q: The Good Girlz deal with real teen issues—everything from boyfriend troubles to jealousy and competition. How do you create stories that are so true to life?

A: By writing reality. I write what I have lived, and what I see teens deal with on an everyday basis.

Q: Do you have a favorite Good Girl? Which one most reminds you of yourself?

A: One of the things I loved about the Good Girlz is that I took a little bit of me and infused it into each character. Then, I added some characteristics I wish I had growing up. For that reason, it's kind of hard to pick a favorite. I love all of them.

Q: Do you think teenage girls have a harder time than teenage boys? If so, why?

A: Definitely, because let's face it, there are different standard levels for the two groups. Certain behavior is accepted and even excused in young men, but young women can really mess up their lives with that same behavior. Then you have the media sending mixed messages about what's hot, what's beautiful, and what guys want. It can add a lot of pressure to teenage girls.

Q: **What were your favorite books and authors growing up? What do you think are the essential ingredients of a best-selling teen novel?**

A: I loved Maya Angelou's *I Know Why the Caged Bird Sings*. And I was a huge Judy Blume and Nancy Drew reader. I think a teen novel needs to be something that keeps teens' interest; after all, books are competing with so many other forms of entertainment. So a bestselling teen book today has to be a page-turner.

Q: **Do you think celebrities and the media influence how teens view competition and being successful in today's world?**

A: We live in a competitive society and the catfights we hear about in Hollywood and the beefs we see rappers having with each other only serve to fuel the competitive fire. I think unfair pressure is placed on teens by telling them that they have to be the best. I don't have a problem with being the best you can, but it's when we add in that "by any means necessary" part as so many people do. We're teaching young people that you should succeed no matter what, no matter who you have to step on to do it. And that, most often, is not a good thing.

Q: What did you learn from your own experience as a television reporter about the balance between work and personal life? Were you ever in a situation where you felt particularly competitive? If so, how did you handle it?

A: I think oftentimes people can get so caught up in their careers, or following their dreams, that they don't realize what's really important—and that's family and love. The TV news business is extremely competitive. We fought all the time for the big story. I'll admit, I was one of those "bulldog reporters." But at the end of the day, none of that mattered. You can be the star one day and fizzle the next. (Just like Camille when they canceled her show.) So it's important to always realize what's really important.

Q: As a parent you are probably concerned about instilling values in your own daughters. How will you accomplish this?

A: Absolutely. I don't want to just write about it, I want to be about it. That means, the things I try to teach in my writings, I definitely will teach in my household. I want to raise strong independent daughters, who make sound moral, ethical, personal, and professional decisions in their own lives. Of course, I'll do that through example, but also by constantly talking to them about staying on the right path.

Q: What will be the next book in your Christian teen series? How do you choose which of the Commandments to focus on next?

A: We are currently at work on the next set of books in the Good Girlz series. I want to make sure we choose an area to focus on that will really touch some lives. So, while we haven't narrowed it down yet, I'm definitely excited about continuing the series.

Questions for Discussions

1. When the original Good Girlz—Camille, Angel, Jasmine, and Alexis—meet their newest member, Tameka Adams, they are turned off by her negative attitude. Camille says, "I'd just stick to the original Good Girlz, the ones I knew were my true friends. I guess we just had no room for outsiders" (page 5). Why do you think the girls don't like Tameka? Does it have anything to do with the fact that she's their group leader's niece? What is the difference between a close-knit group of friends and a "clique"? What would you consider the Good Girlz?

2. Do you think it's a good decision for Angel not to try out for *Teen Talks* because she's now a mom? What does this say about her priorities and life goals? Did she have other options she didn't explore?

3. Competition and lying are two of the major themes in *With Friends Like These*. What is the difference between competition over boys and competition at the television station? When, if ever, is a lie acceptable?

4. Do you think Jasmine has the right to be angry with Alexis for dating Jaquan? Why or why not? Is keeping Jasmine in the dark the same thing as lying to her?

5. Camille and Walter lie to their parents in order to date each other. Is this really necessary? What does this say about their

relationship? Are they dating each other simply to rebel, or are they rebelling because they truly care about each other?

6. Why do you think Tameka uses underhanded tactics, such as giving the girls bad advice and stealing Jasmine's research paper? If she had enough confidence in herself would she still cheat? How do the other girls react?

7. When Alexis and Camille are chosen as the finalists, Camille takes Walter up on his offer to help her get the job. Do you consider this cheating? Do you think she would have been more proud of herself knowing she got the job all on her own? How do the other girls react once they find out?

8. At one point in the competition, Rachel says, "God is at the center of everything we do. . . . We're losing the glue that holds everything together" (page 85). What is Rachel trying to teach the girls about friendship and competition? What are they losing sight of?

9. When the girls believe Alexis had an overdose, they rush to the hospital to be at her side. What does this say about their underlying values and priorities?

10. How does the cancellation of the talk show put things in perspective for Camille? What does she learn about herself and the nature of competition?

Activities to Enhance Your Book Club

Lend a helping hand like the Good Girlz! Find community service projects in your area by logging on to sites such as www.dosomething.org and www.handsonnetwork.org.

If you're the host, read quotes from *With Friends Like These* and see if your friends can guess which characters said them.

Try hosting your own version of *Teen Talks*. Your fellow book club members can come on the show as one of the characters from the book.

Don't miss the first book in this inspiring teen series

Nothing But Drama

Available in paperback from Pocket Books

Turn the page for a preview of *Nothing But Drama* . . .

Camille

I stood outside the small meeting room and checked out the girls inside. There were four other girls there besides me and Angel. One of them, a high yellow girl with a Beyoncé weave, was busy primping in the mirror. Then there was the weird-looking chick dressed in all black sitting in the corner. She looked like a serial killer.

Another girl was looking around nervously like she was scared to death that someone was about to steal her lunch money. Maybe she was scared of Jasmine, who sat two seats down from her. Jasmine's scowl was back and she looked like she would hit anybody who even looked at her the wrong way. She sat in a chair with her arms crossed and her legs gaped wide open like a guy. She looked like she really didn't want to be here.

"I know that feeling," I muttered.

"Did you say something?" Angel whispered. She was the only person who seemed halfway interested in being there.

I shook my head. "Nah, just ready to get this over with. Come on."

I walked into the room with Angel close on my heels. "What's up, y'all?" I was trying to be friendly to these losers as I sat down next to the scary girl.

Angel gave a meek wave and sat down next to me.

Jasmine didn't reply. Neither did Goth girl. Scary girl looked away and Miss Prissy kept flinging her hair.

"I guess these stuck-up girls are too good to speak," I told Angel loud enough for them to hear.

Jasmine sat up in her seat and dropped her arms like she was ready to rumble. "Who you calling stuck-up when you all up in other people's business?"

Now, I know I had just witnessed this girl beat the crap out of a guy, but for some reason I wasn't intimidated. Don't get me wrong, I'm definitely not a fighter, but I'm no punk, either. "If the shoe fits."

Jasmine stood up and started walking toward me. I kept my game face on but I couldn't help but think if she hit me, I was gon' have to grab something and try and knock her out because no way could I win a fistfight with her.

"Now, I know you two are not about to fight up here in the Lord's house."

We all turned toward Rachel, who had just stepped into the meeting room. No one answered her.

"Jasmine, you promised no fighting," Rachel said as she walked into the room. "I go into my office for one minute and walk back out here to find you all at each other's throats before you even know one another's names." Rachel walked to the front of the room and set her Bible and a folder down on the podium. "Rule number one: There will be absolutely no fighting in this church."

"Then you better tell this pint-size freak to leave me alone," Jasmine said as she glared at me.

I had my nerve back now that Rachel was in the room to keep me from getting killed. "I guess everybody would be pint-size to you, you—"

"Enough!" Rachel snapped.

"You better tell her, Miss Rachel," Jasmine said.

"I got this, Jasmine. Sit down." Rachel turned toward me. "You have a seat, too." She waited for both of us to sit back down. "Now, this is not the way I wanted us to get things started. We are in this for the long run, so we might as well all learn to get along." Rachel took a deep breath, then flashed a bright smile. "Let's start by introducing ourselves. I'll go first. Welcome to the first meeting of the Good Girlz. For those of you who don't know, I'm Rachel Adams. I'm the First Lady of Zion Hill and the founder of the Good Girlz. Don't let the name fool you. We're not trying to make you out to be Goody Two-shoes."

I tried not to smile. She must've been reading my mind.

Rachel continued. "But we do want to get you to realize that you are entitled to the good things in life. None of us here are better than anyone else. We all have issues and our goal is to help each other work through them. We'll also take part in some service activities and do our share of giving back to the community."

Rachel clapped her hands together. She was obviously

excited about this program. "We will deal with your issues and discuss ways we can live more godly lives."

I couldn't help but let out a disgusted sigh. Here we go with the preaching.

"But first, let's start by just having everyone give their names. Then we'll come back and let you tell a little about yourself," Rachel continued.

Angel introduced herself first. Then me, then everybody else. The scary-looking girl was Sasha. Tameka was the girl dressed all in black like she was going to a funeral or something. And the diva over there was Alexis.

"Now, let's move on and talk about ourselves." Rachel smiled at us, but I wasn't taking the bait. "When I say we all have issues, I just want you to know that includes me. While I'm a proud First Lady now, and the daughter of a preacher, I ain't always been holy." She stopped and laughed, piquing my interest.

"Even now, it takes a lot of effort for me to walk the straight and narrow. I'm a preacher's kid . . . and you know what they say about preacher's kids."

"Y'all the worst ones," I offered. The other girls laughed along with me. Except for Jasmine. She still had a scowl.

"I don't know about all preachers' kids, but I can tell you this preacher's kid was pretty bad," Rachel said. "Any crazy thing you've done behind a boy, I've already done it. Any disappointment you might have given your parents, been there, done that. So I'm hoping you all will get to the point where you will feel comfortable opening up." Rachel turned toward me. "Your turn. What's your name?"

"Camille Harris."

"Okay, Camille Harris. Where are you from and what made you come here?"

The smile left my face. I didn't want to sit up in church and lie but I still wasn't feeling letting these girls all up in my business. "I'm from the southwest part of Houston. I go to Madison High School and I'm here, umm, because my mom thought it would be good for me."

Rachel looked at me like she knew there was more to the story. "Okay, I'm sure we'll get more in depth later."

I was grateful that she didn't push it and instead moved on to the scary-looking girl.

"And you would be?" Rachel asked.

The girl didn't respond.

"You don't have to be nervous," Rachel said.

She still didn't say anything.

"How about we come back to you?" The girl nodded and Rachel gave her a reassuring smile.

"Tameka, why don't you come out of the corner and come up here and introduce herself."

Goth girl looked like she wanted to crawl up in a hole and die. She reluctantly moved toward the front of the room.

"My name is Tameka. I go to Hightower High School," she all but whispered.

"Tameka is my niece," Rachel said proudly. "She lives in

Missouri City, but she's here because I'm trying to expose her to different things, right?"

Tameka groaned, but didn't say anything.

"She's a little shy," Rachel said. "But we're going to work on that in this group. Right, Tameka?"

Tameka shrugged. Rachel sighed before turning her attention to Angel. "Your turn," Rachel said.

"Hi, I'm Angel. I attend Westbury High School, at least for now, anyway. I don't know if I'm going to stay there, because . . . things aren't going too good for me right now."

Rachel pressed on. "And why aren't things going well?"

Angel sighed. "I, um, I had to move away from my neighborhood."

"Where are your parents?" Alexis asked. I didn't even know she knew how to talk in complete sentences, since she hadn't bothered to say anything more than her name.

Angel looked real uncomfortable. "Me and my mom, well, it's just me." Angel puckered her lips together like she wanted to say more but she kept quiet.

"Oh, snap. I bet she's a runaway," Jasmine said.

"I am not a runaway," Angel protested. She shot Jasmine a mean look. "I'm staying with my sister right now."

"Whatever." Jasmine shrugged. "I just think you need to stop lying, that's all, especially all up in a church."

Angel glared at Jasmine like she couldn't stand her. "My mom didn't want me there. Does that make you feel better?" she snapped.

For once, Jasmine looked apologetic. "Dang, I'm sorry."

"I came here because stuff is tight with my sister and . . ." Angel dropped her hands in her lap and turned toward Rachel. "I was just hoping to win the drawing you were gon' have tonight because I really need the money." She looked like she was trying not to cry.

Rachel walked over to Angel and took her hands as she sat down next to her. "Angel, God doesn't do anything by chance. You are here tonight for a reason. He put that flyer in your hand. He led you here because He knew you need what this group can offer."

I tried not to turn up my nose. What could this group possibly offer besides wasting my time? Stop with all the negativity, this little voice in my head seemed to say. I turned my attention back to Rachel.

"Whatever demons you are wrestling with, we want to help you work them out." Rachel squeezed Angel's hand before standing up and walking back to the front of the room. "Part of our problem in trying to live a Godly life is that we don't know we're being attacked. Drugs, alcohol, whatever drives you away from a Godly life is a tool that the Devil uses to attack you."

I really was not trying to hear a sermon. I was tired and ready to get home. Rachel must've read the look on my face because she said, "And the Devil also messes with our mind so that we can't receive the Word when it's being fed to us." She smiled at me and I immediately felt embarrassed.

"Amen to that."

We all turned toward my mother, who stood in the meeting room doorway. She was wearing a gigantic smile.

"Can you tell them that again?" my mother said.

I couldn't help but groan as my mother walked into the room. She stuck her hand out toward Rachel. "I'm Mrs. Harris, Camille's mother."

Rachel shook her hand. "Nice to meet you."

"Sorry to interrupt, but Mrs. Washington said you'd be finished by seven," my mother said.

Rachel looked down at her watch. "Wow, I can't believe time has flown by that quickly." She looked at all of us. "We will wrap up for today but think on these two things. I want us to create a bond here and that means you all will communicate outside of the group. I want everyone to make sure your numbers are correct on this paper." Rachel handed a piece of paper to me. I reluctantly took it.

"I'll make copies for everyone and have them at the next meeting. I also need to give away that door prize I advertised," Rachel said.

Angel perked up.

"Normally, I would do a drawing," Rachel said. "But I want our first lesson of our group to be one of selflessness. How about we all agree to give it to Angel?"

Angel smiled as she nervously looked around.

"Anybody have a problem with that?" Rachel asked.

Me, Alexis, and Tameka shook our heads. Jasmine shrugged.

Before I knew it, I found myself saying, "I think that sounds like a good idea."

"Then it's a done deal." Rachel reached into her Bible and pulled out an envelope. She handed it to Angel. "I know you said you came for the money, but I hope you'll come back because you like being with us."

Angel blushed. "I will."

Rachel dismissed the group and we all headed for the door. Just a few minutes ago I was itching to get out of here, but as I looked at my mom standing in the doorway with that big stupid grin, I realized my two hours there weren't so bad after all.